LOVE BRAIN
& OTHER
MINEFIELDS

ALAN COLLENETTE

SWANTORINI PRESS

For the Black Swan.

With grateful thanks.

Your flair and spirit

helped shape

these pages.

Table of Contents

Foreword

THIS DIVERSE COLLECTION OF Alan Collenette's work navigates the spectrum of human experience, lurching from the absurdly comedic to the profoundly tragic, and covering everything in between. Within these stories, essays, and poems, there is a heartfelt reverence for women – a celebration of their impact and an expression of admiration from a male perspective. At the same time, many pieces wander into entirely unrelated territories. Tracing one man's passage through the sorrows and delights he encounters at various stages of his life.

A recurring motif is a hilarious and exaggerated commentary on the challenges men face in trying to match the emotional and intellectual intelligence of women. It's as if men are bewildered artisans, rummaging through life's unlit toolshed in pursuit of the right tools, whether for the bedroom or elsewhere, only to find themselves baffled and outfoxed.

PART ONE

THE HEART'S MINEFIELD

MEN'S WORTHLESS PLAYBOOK

Chapter 1

Mister Speedy

I T IS 1996. I am forty. My wife, Anne, whom I miss a great deal, dumped me and now lives cross the street.

I am dating in secret through the personal ads. Anne's boyfriend, a large and much younger man called Dick (his real name), has forearms like ham hocks and a small irritating dog that pees on my hubcaps.

One morning, awake as usual in the pre-dawn, I reach a new low, and begin picturing inscriptions for my gravestone. The wording lurches from personal ad (when personal ads in newspapers were a thing) to epitaph:

DWM

(Dead White Male)

Nice man.

Good worker.

Fell asleep in his fortieth year.

Wife got away.

Time has reformatted our parting scene in my mind, so that it plays something like this:

I am in my home office in the garage, vaguely aware that dinner is spoiling in the oven.

"Julian, you love your job more than me, and we are strangers. I am leaving you."

I look up from the computer, interrupting an email to head office.

"I could quit my job."

"You'd be broke. A broke husband is even worse than a stranger."

"What about a broke stranger?"

"This is a delay tactic, Julian. I have to go now."

"Please don't leave me." My pager beeps, and I look down to see who is calling. I write the client's number on a pad.

"My boyfriend's waiting outside. I have to go."

"Boyfriend?"

"Hello! The guy I've been sleeping with for six months."

A cruel strike, but it helps me to focus. My mobile phone rings. I hesitate briefly, then ignore it. In a fog, it comes to me. All those late nights when I would come back from the office to find the bed empty, Anne's car not outside. The sound of her key in the latch at dawn. Her getting in bed beside me, reeking of an unfamiliar cologne. Her slightly torn dress and tiny panties slung over the chair rail, bathed in the first rays of the rising sun. But now I say nothing, wearing what I suppose is the stunned look of a caught fish in a bucket.

"Oh, what?" she asks. "Did you think I was walking the dog all those nights?"

"You wouldn't have needed the car to walk the dog."

"Julian, we don't *have* a dog."

My job doesn't seem at all important now, and I am home early most days. But I'm not stupid; overwork was only one reason she left me. The other was that I am an awkward man; not smooth at all. To women, smooth is sexy. Smooth can't miss.

"Julian," she once said to me, "You are a sweet man, but you are not smooth. Not smooth at all. You are an awkward man."

That was the day I had picked up the laundry for her. I balanced the bulging clothes basket on the car roof, opened the door, forgot it was there, and drove home. As I retraced the route later, articles of Anne's cherished lingerie, presumably now also cherished by Dick, festooned the roads and sidewalks of the neighborhood.

In our kitchen, as a monument to my ineptitude, a jar of preserves sat for some years unopened, on top of the fridge. Anne had asked me to open it at one time. That is what men do. We open preserve jars for our wives. They much prefer this ability to a skilled Sexsmith. Even if the jar is sealed with an industrial strength adhesive, it is a basic requirement. This is how we garner respect.

"No problem," I had said, but it was. I took a crack at it occasionally, when she wasn't looking, but its contents remained secure.

So now Anne lives across the street, I mean directly opposite, on our cul-de-sac. In the divorce settlement, both of us too stubborn to yield, she kept our house, which we mortgaged, and I bought the identical one opposite, using the mortgage proceeds as a down payment. I know I may not get her back, but I think I may have just a chance if I can get her to see me in a new light; to believe suddenly that, underneath this lingerie-spreading, defeated-by-preserve-jars exterior, there has always lurked a smooth, dignified Julian.

I call in sick, yet again, and take the day off so I can talk things over with my therapist. She says that the concept of smooth is a male construct. Men, she says, worry about batting averages, sex, and smoothness, while women focus on the important issues. Like time spent on the relationship. Smooth, my therapist says firmly, is of no consequence to women like Anne. I do not argue. She is wrong, but I don't want to embarrass a professional.

The personal ad is serving its purpose. It has enabled me to parade a string of women past Anne's front door on their way to and from dates with me. It is now early evening, and the girl who, on the phone claimed to be of a "compatible" age, pulls into my driveway. She is pretty much a teenager. I am horrified. She could be my daughter. This is an emergency.

If Anne sees this high schooler, it will not be good. Anne drives up to her house and climbs out of her car.

My date opens her car door. I press it shut. She tries once more, but I lean against the door. Anne walks over to me.

"Julian, you're home early. Again. That's nice to see. Whatever happened to Mister All Work and No Play?" She is about to head back across the road when she gestures toward my date's car and says, "Why don't you let the poor thing out, Julian? If you want to *do* anything, you'd better hurry. It's a school night."

It is not a good evening, and I bring it to an early close. My date takes the hint right after dinner when I mention my brave (but imaginary) struggle with herpes. In our mutual haste to say goodbye, I shut my hand in her car door. Once in bed, exhausted from trying to be attentive while thinking entirely about Anne, my fingers throb relentlessly.

I picture Anne smiling at me. I shiver. She's the only fantasy I ever had. I am too busy to chat. My hand rests casually on the roof of a limo. Inside, there are two well-known models I am chaperoning to a nightclub. A rear door is open, with one of the model's legs protruding, her toe tapping impatiently on the ground. Anne stares at me, her incredible green eyes glinting in the sun's last rays.

"Julian, I know I should let go of you, but I just have to say one thing."

I smile politely, checking my Bulgari timepiece, and say impatiently,

"Can this wait?"

"Please, just give me a second, Julian." She sounds almost desperate. I sigh.

"Very well. If it won't take too long."

"Beside you," she blurts out, "other men...like...well...Dick. You're so *masterful*." I feel her sweet breath on my cheek.

"Yes. I know Anne. Thank you."

I don't look back as I climb into the car, and the door shuts behind me.

Dick's dog is a Corgi, the same breed as the Queen of England's, he boasts. The Queen calls her dogs Sir Thomas Moore and Lord Percy. Dick's is called Mister Speedy. In England, the Queen's corgis strut neatly at the monarch's heels, their groomed and muscled bodies sheathed in tartan coats with matching tail covers, heads high. Bred for their powerful bladder control, they have never been recorded peeing on the hubcaps of the Royal Daimler.

Mister Speedy is neither groomed nor muscled. His overall appearance is that of a polyester cushion left in the washer/dryer for three consecutive cycles at 1,000 degrees. He does not strut neatly. I have watched him as he heads for my '75 VW Beetle with a lurching motion, his belly weighed down by a massive bladder, scraping along the asphalt toward my hubcaps like a fire plane coming in to dump water on a blaze.

The next evening at twilight, while putting my garbage out, I become enraged for the tenth consecutive evening at the sight of the pitted yellow hubcaps on the VW. Something inside me snaps, and on impulse, I decide to act. Furtively, I steal across the street to Anne's house, outside which sits Dick's new Lexus, newly waxed and glinting in the moonlight, with its darkly tinted windows, and its spoiler erect like a scorpion's tail. Just parked, the cooling engine still mutters under the hood. With the car between me and the house, my eye on the front door, I unzip my fly and take aim at the Lexus's driver-side wheel. Anxiety grips me, as it does when called upon to give a urine sample to the nurse at the doctor's office. Nothing emerges. I focus on waterfalls and alpine streams gurgling across pebbles. Surely, I can out-pee Mister Speedy? At that moment, two things happen simultaneously. From the back seat of the Lexus, Mister Speedy starts to bark uncontrollably, and the front door of the house opens to reveal Anne, looking directly at the Lexus and squinting to adjust to the fading light. In an unfortunate coincidence, my stubborn friend decides to respond to the stimulus of the alpine imagery and lets loose a fearsome jet of urine, as if he had been called upon to spray a burning building. I attempt to stop midstream, at the same time as zipping my pants, but such a delicate maneuver is beyond the abilities of my bruised fingers to manage. I duck down in the hope that Anne will not be able to see me over the car roof. I hear her advancing footsteps above the yelping and skittering of Mister Speedy.

"Speedo" calls Anne, "Speed, Speed, Speedo." But the hound's face is glued to the inside of the car's window in front of me. Anne's feet crunch on the driveway as she rounds the hood of the Lexus to my side. I dive to the soaking ground and crawl underneath. I hear Anne open the car door. There is a skittering of paws, and in a second a Corgi face appears under the car, pressed up against mine, all dog breath and teeth.

"Dick!" shouts Anne toward the house. "Speedo's cornered something under the car."

Presently, I am staring into the beam of Dick's flashlight and pulling myself out from under the car. I search for an explanation. None immediately springs to mind. Mister Speedy's muzzle sniffs at my drenched crotch like a vacuum on a rug. Dick towers over me, one huge ham hock around Anne's shoulders. I picture him holding Anne's preserve jar in the palm of one hand, not a hint of strain on his face as he removes the lid with one masterful twist of the wrist.

"Julian?" Anne is saying, "I *thought* it was you." Dick smirks and heads for the house. Mister Speedy follows him with a victorious, lilting waddle, his stomach scuffing the gravel driveway. The front door closes behind the dog and his master.

There I am, standing a few feet from Anne, my hands clasped in front of my crotch, face burning with embarrassment, when something wonderful happens. Anne comes up close to me, smiles, and says, "Julian, you know, I kind of miss you and your silly ways."

I can tell from her tone that she really means what she says, and it comes to me at this moment that my understanding of women may not be entirely complete.

Chapter 2
Ingling

I T WAS ONLY LATER, during a post-mortem the following spring, that it was to occur to Adam that it should have been illegal to make plans for a winter trip to England when you are enveloped in a California summer; just as when you are deeply in love, it should be illegal to plan a marriage: you are making a decision out of context.

Adam's mother lived in London, where he was from. She was raised during rationing in wartime Britain, the era of thrice boiled ham hock soup and walking everywhere to save petrol for the boys at the front.

His wife, Sue Anne, lived with him in California. Sue Anne had been bred in the America of JFK, T-bones the size of pianos, and Cadillacs where the needle on the fuel gauge moved from right to left faster than the windshield wipers.

Adam understood and admired these women. Sometimes he felt like a sports fan who idolized two teams with completely opposite playing styles. He enjoyed the thrifty relish with which his mother chewed everything forty times and walked two miles to save ten pence for a postage stamp;

the way she would wait outside the butcher's shop until just before closing time to buy cheaply the cuts from unmentionable parts of sheep that would otherwise be thrown in the dustbins.

He respected Sue Anne's rebellion against the excesses of her early diet; her tireless searches for healthy food, her quest for ever more organic produce. If he had been asked what the two women had in common, he would have answered that they were equally stubborn; programmed to defend an untenable position long after other women would have conceded victory. And a fierce temper.

It was the height of summer in California. Adam and Sue Anne were sitting in a café overlooking the slopes of the Napa Valley, a light breeze blowing through the vineyards, the sun just a little too hot. Suddenly, out of left field, the idea of Christmas came to him.

Adam had always believed that Christmas was an absurd time to travel vast distances to see relatives. Everyone either has the flu or is morbidly afraid of getting it. If you were seeking a miserable climate, Adam believed you would always select London in December. This was why he had moved to California in the first place. In London at this time of year the days were always gray and leaden, conveying a feeling of recent bereavement and of disappointment, suggestive of lost empires and cheating monarchs, an atmosphere so oppressive that when it began to darken at 3:30 each day, it was a merciful relief. Adam actually liked California at Christmas time.

He looked forward to the mornings when the fog would lift to reveal a sparkling ocean backlit by a cheery winter sun. Still, duty beckoned.

"Mother's 75 this year," he began. "I feel bad that she hardly knows Emily. Last time mother saw her she was one, and now she's at preschool already." He could feel Sue Anne bristle. She already knew where this was heading.

"Let's have your *mom* come visit." The accent on *mom* was not lost on Adam. The well-worn cliché of mother-in-law vs. wife that must have beset cavemen at the dawn of mankind.

"What about England at Christmas? Emily would love the plane ride. We can go to Hamleys in Regent Street and sit on Santa's knee. Carols at Westminster Abbey."

Sue Anne winced. "All that tea. It's *always* teatime. Wake up tea, breakfast tea, elevenses...,"

"Even you drink tea sometimes."

"Not all day. Tea with lunch, afternoon tea, tea before bed. Stomach problems and stained teeth."

"The British built an empire on tea."

"Oh, of course. The Falkland Islands?"

"Mother's been so lonely since dad died. She could use our company."

"I feel bad for your mother, but if she didn't smoke, your dad would still be with her. It's the rare husband that thrives on secondhand smoke."

"She's promised not to smoke while we're there."

"And you *always* side with your *mother*. Last time, it was a nightmare. A siege. God, I can feel it now-that queasy, outnumbered feeling. No cavalry coming over the crest of the ridge to rescue me; for that matter, no ridge even. Just that tiny cold house. Stodgy food. Cigarette smoke. No fresh vegetables. Rain every day. Traffic. Fumes."

"You sound like a travelogue. You should write tourist brochures."

"Anyhow, your mother doesn't like me. She's always talking about your brother's wife and kids, and how smart they were to settle in London, and how America is full of vulgar fat people who talk about money and spend it on cars and video games instead of their kids' education."

"She doesn't mean it. I will have a word with her. She is very fond of you." Adam had by this time resorted to outright lying.

"And her cooking. How can you even think of exposing Emily to all that overcooked fat and pesticide residue?"

"We'll eat out a lot."

"Where? At the International House of Overcooked Mad Cow?" She puckered her lips and screwed up her nose in disgust. Half the food in England sounds like the kind of uncomfortable medical condition you are embarrassed even to tell your doctor about. She imitated an English waiter. "'Would madam care for the Toad in the Hole, or the Spotted Dick?'"

Adam tried not to laugh, but Sue Anne had him in stitches. He got a grip on himself and decided guilt was his only hope.

"...the autumn of mother's life...would not forgive ourselves if anything should happen before... deny my mother the pleasure of seeing her only granddaughter." When Sue Anne finally agreed, however, Adam was left with the uneasy feeling that it was a Pyrrhic victory. A ghastly carnage would follow.

Even before they got on the plane, all three of them had colds. On the 12-hour flight, as other people coughed and hacked into the recirculating air system, their own colds turned into severe colds, and they became tense and snippy. Emily stood on her seat and cast animal shadows into the movie projector beam with her hands. She thought this improved Flubber immensely. The other passengers disagreed. They glared at Adam and his family for the rest of the trip. Flight attendants gave frequent and unsolicited parenting advice.

Pre-dawn Heathrow featured a two-mile-long walk along a motionless 'moving' walkway, culminating in a sniffer dog search of their baggage. Sue Anne's organic apples and Tarantula-poison-free bananas were confiscated by a sallow-faced customs official.

"Vitamin-starved weasel," she hissed.

Adam hailed a taxi. The driver studied the coughing, squabbling family unit, hesitated for a few moments and then beckoned the people behind us in the queue to jump into his cab. Twenty minutes later he finally persuaded a taxi driver to take them, after whispering to him that the tip would be double the meter reading.

Adam's mother met them at the threshold of her tiny London house just after daybreak. Emily looked up from Sue Anne's arms and said, "Who's that lady? I don't like her," before bursting into tears and hiding her head.

Sue Anne and her mother-in-law struggled with an uneasy hug.

"I'll make you a nice cup of tea," said Adam's mother.

"I'll pass, thanks," said Sue Anne hastily.

Avoiding eye contact with Sue Anne, Adam said, "I'll have one mum."

Up in the bedroom Sue Anne, Adam and Emily inspected the two single beds, with worn out springs, thrust together, a high, hard ridge between. There was room to walk around the bed, but only sideways. The curtains smelled of cigarette smoke, as did the frayed bath towels that Adam's mother had laid on the end of the bed. Adam cringed as Emily began whining loudly in a voice that must have been clearly audible from the kitchen downstairs.

"I don't like Ingling. I don't like that lady. I want to go home."

"This was your idea, Adam. She's *your* mother. If it was up to me, I'd be on the next plane back."

The visit careened from crisis to crisis. Adam's mother smoked in the garden, but the fumes wafted inside. The household was awash in tea the whole time. Sue Anne explained to Adam's mother that although England still clung to the misguided belief that it was a great nation, the country was in the dark ages in a few areas, including, but not limited to, food, pollution, and home furnishings.

Adam's mother explained to Sue Anne that, as a girl, Adam's sister Annie had really been quite advanced at Emily's age, and wasn't Emily able to do jigsaws on her own yet, and didn't all those American Disney videos have an effect on children's' intellectual growth? And wasn't it America that invented fizzy drinks in aluminum cans that gave you Alzheimer's? And wasn't it time that Emily got baptized? And had Adam gone to church at all since he met Sue Anne?

Adam's pre-trip vision had been of happy chatter around Yule logs set against the faint background of Christmas carols and excited faces. This was now replaced by abject despair. The only relief was the knowledge that the central conflict did not really involve him. He was a spectator rather than a participant in the struggle. He began to suspect, though, that he would, sooner or later, be called to arms.

The denouement came on Christmas day as Adam's mother was preparing dinner. Sue Anne was pretending to show willing, circling the kitchen with insincere offerings to help. Emily was in the living room, watching an American version of Winnie the Pooh that Adam's mother had thought was "rather modern and a departure from the original classic that Mr. Milne had intended. Why sit inside watching videos? Why not a day trip to, say, Stonehenge for fresh air and a proper education?" Adam was trying to concentrate on the *Sunday Times* Christmas edition crossword, but out of the corner of his eye he was watching Sue Anne's facial expressions. He knew that look only too well. She was looking on with mounting color in her cheeks as her mother-in-law prepared a humongous turkey for dinner. As she had suspected, the bird was not free range. Its immense rubbery body quivered on the table as Adam's mother stuffed and trussed it. It looked to be a bird that had spent its life in dark places, eating and pooping. Adam speculated that it had probably never stood on its own two legs without support from a row of equally flaccid companions propping one and other up on either side.

Sue Anne was, Adam could tell, about to blow. His mother, oblivious in her full Christmas stride, was unaware of this.

"Adam, you like my turkey, don't you?" Adam feigned intense concentration on the crossword.

"My turkey, Adam. You've always had seconds every Christmas since you were a little boy. You must like it; don't you?"

"What is a word, meaning December holiday, that has nine letters beginning with a C? Last letter is an S?"

"You're avoiding the question, Adam. Is there something wrong with my turkey?"

The game was up. Sue Anne left the dugout and came onto the field.

"Adam doesn't eat turkey raised in an incubator." She presented this as an unchallengeable statement of fact.

"Can't he speak for himself?"

"Mother. I love your turkey. It's just..."

"He wants to live to middle age. Do you know what they feed those turkeys? Do you think they peck casually at scatterings of assorted wild grains in open meadow land? They eat pellets. Chemical pellets with ingredients like Trysorbate Number 12. Aluminum Absorbatol. Laboratory rats see those ingredients coming and commit suicide against the cage bars rather than be forced to sample them."

Sue Anne put her hand on the turkey's shiny, basted back and squeezed its lumpy flesh. She shook it so that it wobbled.

"If this wasn't labeled *food* in supermarkets," she finally thundered, "if instead our hunter-gatherer ancestors had come upon it on, say, a forage in prehistoric Salisbury Plain, in the shadow of Stonehenge, it would not have occurred to them to consider it as food. They wouldn't have dared offer it as a sacrifice to the gods for fear of it being returned to them with a divine command to *eat it yourself*. Adam doesn't eat this garbage."

The older woman now put her hand on the turkey and wrapped it around the right-side drumstick.

"This is *my* house. Adam is *my* son. My turkey has always been good enough for him, and he has grown up big and strong and healthy enough that I see it didn't take you more than a split second to seize on him after his divorce and snap him up. You didn't then seem to feel the need to conduct an historical nutritional profile and if you're so bloody healthy how come you have streaming colds when you come here?"

"With a house this draughty, you might as well save the money and leave off the roof and doors. How could anyone be healthy at this temperature?"

"I don't feel the cold. Maybe it's because I eat warming healthy food and don't sit around in pampered surroundings provided to you by my son, watching soap operas and drinking soft drinks out of a recyclable can."

Adam watched as Sue Anne's hand slid down to the left side drumstick, gripping it firmly. The juice was oozing around her wedding ring. Sue Anne moved towards his mother.

"I am not eating this thing and nor is my family."

"It's *my* family. Adam is *my* son, Emily's *my* granddaughter and they will eat what I cook." Adam's mother began pulling on her drumstick.

The two women were suddenly standing in the middle of the kitchen floor, each heaving on a drumstick, both standing their ground. Their hands kept slipping so that first Sue Anne and then Adam's mother changed hands to get a better grip and to shake off the grease.

Suddenly, with a tearing sound, the leg his mother was holding tore free from the rotund butter ball, and she staggered across the kitchen, coming to rest against the fridge, which wobbled with the impact. At the same time, Sue Anne flew backwards across the room into one of the dining chairs, clutching the entire bird minus one leg, and slumped into the chair with it.

Adam could no longer keep up the pretense of the crossword. He looked at Sue Anne, hugging the bird as though it might escape if she freed it, and then at his mother, who was red in the face and brandishing the lone turkey leg. He began to laugh. It was the relief of not being one of the combatants. It was the absurdity of the two women for whom he had the most respect in the world, for whom he would gladly have risked his life, clutching turkey parts and fighting for their claims to be matriarch.

Suddenly, in unison, both Sue Anne and Adam's mother began to laugh too. At first the laughter was a gentle sound, accompanied by a rolling of the shoulders and a slight shuddering. Then it became a loud snorting from his mother, her glorious white hair standing like a plume on her shaking head, and tears in Sue Anne's pretty green eyes. Sue Anne got up, set the turkey down on the table, and walked towards Adam's mother, holding out her arms, as the older woman came forward and willingly accepted the hug. By now Adam had cast the crossword completely aside and watched in awe as Sue Anne and his mother tried to reassemble the turkey, Sue Anne clutching it again in her arms and his mother brandishing a strand of twine and pressing the drumstick back against its yielding flesh. For a long while, the three of them just laughed, until they were tired and their stomachs ached.

When the room subsided again into quiet, it came to Adam that, as a spectator, if you support both teams, you can't lose.

Chapter 3

Paradise Motors

IT WAS 1997 AND Charlie was in the twilight of his career, the last mile of the freeway. He knew no one could sell cars quite like he could. This particular sale, however, was not going well. The young couple with the kid just would not stop grinding him down. You'd think they'd be tired of this by now.

"This isn't some *Japanese* car, you know," Charlie said. "This is a Ford. Made in Dearborn. Unlike the offshore competition, the Ford is value engineered not to come apart in heavy rain. Over here, we have this magnificent Sunblush Yellow Ford Sundance. Every time we get one in, we have customers fighting with each other to buy it. These babies are the fastest selling cars I have seen in all my thirty years in the business."

Charlie turned and walked towards the car. "Here, Ann, Dave, follow me and I'll let you sit in her."

Charlie turned around and saw that neither of them was following. He came back to where they had been standing.

"My business partner is Japanese," the wife said.

"Shrewd businesspeople, the Japanese," Charlie said quickly.

"And anyway," she continues, "if those Fords sell so quickly, why is that one covered with dust?"

"$11,750 is the price we've decided on," she continued. "That's the most we will pay for this car." Women are irrational. They never play fair. Men will pretty much pay the sticker price. Get a woman involved and fair play goes out the window.

"I doubt that's do-able," Charlie lied. "It'd put me 10% below wholesale, never mind the options and the Valu Pak." He looked from husband to wife and back again, maintaining ruthless eye contact. "Dave, Ann. I like you. I'll go ask my sales manager."

Jim Carter was the sales manager. His dad, Bruce Carter, had been a Presbyterian Minister before he started the dealership. Bruce Carter Ford sold lemons at inflated prices behind a cloak of religious respectability. Crosses hung on the walls at strategic locations, visible to customers from every part of the showroom. A plaque hung above the cash desk:

And on the eighth day,

God created zero percent financing.

Although Charlie was a heathen, he took full advantage of the scam. If Jim Carter's old man hadn't owned the dealership, Charlie figured Jim couldn't even have landed a job selling newspapers...a kid with the charisma of a rusty Subaru and a mind like a five speed Pinto with four neutrals. If his dad only knew how much time Jim spent playing tennis with his old college buddies when he was supposed to be at church or selling cars.

Charlie walked into Carter's office at the rear of the dealership, grabbing a giant glazed donut from the customer snack bar on the way. He turned, bit into the donut, and looked back through the one-way glass at the showroom floor. The wife was tapping out some figures with the point of a pencil on a hand-held calculator. The husband, the baby hung in a cloth carrier dangling from his neck, was shaking his head steadily from side to side. Charlie closed the door to Carter's office.

"Baby Boomers," Charlie said. "The broad is acting like *she* is paying for the car, and her wienerdick husband won't put his foot down." Charlie patted the crown of his toupee.

"And," he continued, "they're hoping to make up for everything they pissed away in the eighties out of my commission on this one stupid car." Charlie polished the toe of one cowboy boot on the calf of his plaid pants.

Carter was pacing about in white shorts and an open-necked tennis shirt. It was almost time for his three o'clock game. Charlie grimaced at the sight of the crucifix tangled in the hairs on his scrawny chest.

"Have you remembered the basics?" Carter asked smugly. "Are you calling her '*madam*'? Remember, ladies make many of the decisions these days...that's why we professionals show them respect."

"Save it, sonny. I forgot more about selling than you will ever learn. When you're old enough to wear long pants, I'll teach you some of the basics." *The kid's clueless* he said to himself. If he'd been born a car, he'd have been part of an immediate factory recall.

"You want to keep this job?" Carter sneered.

"Don't tempt me."

Carter paused to let this sink in.

"Remember, Charlie, repeat the features one by one each time before you answer a question about pricing."

"Features? Like what? Windshield wipers? Wheels? Jimmy, this car is totally stripped. It has the kind of features you'd expect if you'd left it for a month under the freeway in East Oakland."

"Charlie, this is an American car. These people are Americans. Appeal to their patriotism."

This was beginning to wear Charlie down. There was a sudden fluttering under his ribs like a bird against the bars of a cage. His paunch felt as heavy as a medicine ball. He regretted, momentarily, the lifetime of all-u-can-eat seafood binges. Lobsters drenched in butter. Oysters launching themselves off the half shell and luging down his throat. He leaned on the door handle for a full minute.

"You O.K., Charlie?"

"Yes," he said, catching his breath. "Stupid people get to me, is all." The double meaning was wasted on Carter.

"Customers may seem stupid sometimes, Charlie. But remember, they're always right."

Charlie was thinking that Carter was a total moron. Straight out of the fifties Fuller Brush salesman's manual.

"And, Charlie... best wipe the donut glaze off your chin before you go back out there."

Charlie wiped his face with the flat of his hand and strode back towards the couple, his expression oozing concern. "Dave, Ann, the Sales Manager says there has been a mistake. This particular car has in fact been... how shall I put it... spoken for."

"Pardon?" said the woman, glaring at him and then looking at her husband for support. Her husband took the cue.

"You know, I'm *a lawyer*," he said with menace.

Well, would you be upset if I didn't bow? Charlie formed the words but didn't say them.

Mister Wienerdick went on.

"You have entered into a good faith oral contract with us." The kid in the sling woke up and belched.

"You should know that we will demand, and receive, satisfaction. I hope you have insurance."

"Dave," said Charlie, softly, "another five hundred would secure this automobile."

"How so?' said the wife. "You just said the car was sold."

"Not sold, exactly, Ann. More spoken for, you might say."

"Spoken for?" she said. "Just who was it that did the speaking, and how will $500 make them unspeak?"

The kid was blowing raspberries at Charlie from the safety of the papoose sling.

Charlie smiled to himself. Every sale has its climax. Unless the customers get angry, you can't tell if you've pushed them to the limit, can you?

"Dave, Ann, let me clarify this with the Sales Manager," Charlie said. He scrambled back to the safety of Carter's office.

"Why in hell did you tell them it was sold?" Carter asked.

"It's a bluff," said Charlie.

"A bluff? It's a boldfaced lie."

"Look, mister ethics, this is sales. Hello! You got to scare a customer into thinking they lost the car before they really want it. Until you do that, for all they know the car will still be here when Jesus comes back to earth."

"Don't blaspheme."

"I was going on to say that when Jesus does come back, he won't buy some rice burner. He'll buy an American car."

"Well, he sure won't buy it through you," Carter snorted. "He'll want an honest deal."

"Maybe so. But more to the point, Einstein, why would the hero of the biggest selling book of all time, a man who can walk on water and rise from the dead, choose a Ford Sundance? Face it, he wouldn't shop here."

Charlie was thinking that they were probably both in denial. Jesus would buy Japanese for sure. He'd be a comparison shopper. He'd need reliable transport for getting about between miracles. It would have a fish bumper sticker and a roof rack big enough to accommodate a cross. And he might just buy a ragtop. Superstars always buy convertibles. Charlie forced his mouth into a grin as wide as the radiator grille of a fifty-five Corvette, and walked back towards the couple, his hand held out for the husband to shake, but the husband hesitated. Charlie pried the husband's hand out from under the baby's bottom and shook it vigorously. He had begun to sweat, so he wiped his brow with his hand, and the smell of dirty diaper, mingled with donut glaze, almost knocked him over.

"Dave, Ann, congratulations!" he said. The assumptive close. He regretted that his own hand was just a tad sticky from the glaze.

"On what?" the husband asked, again resisting the handshake by keeping his hand limp.

"On account of you and Ann now being...," Charlie hung onto the lawyer's hand like pliers on a rusty engine bolt. "Dave, you and Ann are now the proud owners of the car of your dreams. The Sales Manager called the other customer. He agreed to bow out in view of the extra $500 you and I agreed on to break the ice."

"Wait a minute," said the wife, "we didn't agree..."

"Dave. Ann. *Please* don't tell me you've changed your mind." Charlie kept on smiling, holding the lawyer's hand. He swiveled his eyes from the wife and back again to the husband in rotation. They were going to fight him. Time to beat a retreat.

"OK, tell you what...I'll waive the $500, on account of the misunderstanding."

The couple exchanged glances. "So we're back at the price we offered?" asked the wife. "In that case, in view of that, I suppose we can proceed."

Not allowing them to be alone again even for a second in case they conferred, Charlie finished the paperwork and got their deposit check.

On his way home, the suspension of Charlie's red Mustang seemed to smooth out the bumps in the road like a warm iron running over wrinkled bed sheets. He was trying to cheer himself up by thinking about his substantial commission when the flutter in his ribcage returned.

The bird's wings had turned into talons. The claws tore at the lining of his chest, and the pressure made him slump over the wheel. He breathed deeply and held still. The tearing in his ribs regained ferocity and reached an unbearable crescendo and then, suddenly, all the pain vanished. The road and the steering wheel lost significance, and a calmness consumed everything. Past seafood dinners began to flash through his mind. A parade of lobsters strolled by walking erect on their tails and applying butter to themselves as if it were sunscreen. A choir of oysters sang *Amazing Grace* from a coral bandstand, opening and closing their shells like the mouths of gospel singers.

He blinked and sat up straight. He realized he must have dozed off. To his relief, his hands were still on the wheel, and the car was floating along effortlessly. Completely without effort, in fact. The motor made no sound. The prancing horse at the end of the car's long hood reeled in the wide, sunny freeway ahead. A road sign appeared at the curb:

PREPARE TO STOP GATE AHEAD

Something was very strange. Very wrong. The road was unfamiliar. A thick fog descended and hugged the car, as if he were driving through a cloud. He shivered. He pulled up in front of a massive gate that spanned the full width of the road. It was made of a gold-colored metal, encrusted with pearls of extraordinary size; each one at least 2 inches in diameter. His spirits lifted slightly at the sight of the pearls. Oh, for a taste of the oysters that accompanied them.

At one side of the gate was a toll booth that looked like a sentry box. A sign above it said:

PLEASE CHECK IN AT TOLL BOOTH

The gate keeper was perched on a stool outside. His baseball cap said, *Pearly Gates Inspection Point*, and the badge on the lapel of his overalls read *Saint Peter*.

Charlie sat transfixed in his seat. So, this was death. The weigh station at the final off ramp. He sat motionless for what seemed like hours. When he had finally pulled himself together, he climbed out of the car and held out his hand, flashing the Corvette grille smile.

"Hi, Pete. My name's Charlie. I'm all out of change for the toll. Can I owe you?"

Saint Peter ignored his outstretched hand and looked at him like a customs official at the Mexican border.

"You already paid the toll. Our job is to figure out if it was sufficient."

Charlie was gripped with the same feeling as the time he was pulled over for D.U.I., knowing he was right on the limit.

"What if it wasn't enough?"

"You don't get into The Kingdom."

"Then what?"

"Back that way." Saint Peter pointed to a steep road that led to a tunnel and veered down to Charlie's right. There was a metal emblem over the tunnel entrance, and at first he thought it was a Maserati's hood ornament. Then it dawned on him that the three-pronged fork meant something else. White paint on the tarmac said:

DO NOT REVERSE

SEVERE TIRE DAMAGE MAY OCCUR

"It's one *hell* of a road," added the Saint.

Charlie shuddered. Then he fancied he caught a slight twinkle in Saint Peter's eye.

The Saint flipped open a laptop computer with a harp logo on the keyboard and punched in a few commands. He sucked his teeth and sighed.

"It's marginal," he said finally.

"What is, Pete?"

"Your record."

"I was nice to my mother. Mostly."

"Save your breath, Charles."

"I never lied to a customer. Unless I absolutely had to."

"Charles. It's not me you have to convince. It's up to the Boss."

Saint Peter pointed to a small shed on the path that ran behind the toll booth. It was set into the wire fence that led to the gate, and separated Charlie's side from The Kingdom.

Charlie watched as a winged valet climbed behind the wheel of the Mustang, folded his wings over into the back seat, and parked the car in the lot behind the toll booth. Charlie fumbled in his pocket for a tip but could only produce a ball of plaid lint. Saint Peter shook his head pityingly and motioned Charlie towards the shed.

As Charlie was about to enter, a Toyota Tercel, with more filler than bodywork, skidded to a halt on the other side of the fence, throwing up a cloud of dust. Charlie went into the interview room and sat down in the chair on his side of the glass partition that bisected it. He heard the Tercel driver slam the car door and enter the room with rapid footfalls. She sat down in the chair opposite.

She was Japanese and was drinking from a commute mug with a slogan on the side:

I'M THE BOSS.

EVEN WHEN I'M WRONG, I'M RIGHT.

"Sorry," she said. "Traffic."

She had a kind face and a sparkling smile. Charlie must have looked confused.

"I know, I know," she said. "You thought Jesus would be a man. Well, he's a she. And I'm her. So get over yourself."

Charlie reached deep within himself for composure. "Madam, if I may say so, that's one hell of a relief. My fate in the hands of a man-now that would be scary. I mean women are so much more levelheaded. Rational. So much... fairer. That must be why they call you the fair sex."

"Charlie... "

"Before we get to your decision- and I know, with all of your experience and your, your fairness, you will make the right choice-before we get to that, let me just run over a few of the benefits of having me as a citizen."

"Charlie... "

"First, I was always good to my mother. Right to the last. After she was gone, I splurged on the 4'x6' marble headstone instead of the more modest, yet quite attractive, stone cross. She will be overjoyed to see me."

Charlie intensified his eye contact and cranked open the smile.

"Second, if you have trouble selling off your old fleet cars-and between you and me ma'am the Jap... Japanese cars have always had a problem with resale value-I'm your man. Matter of fact, I happened to notice, madam, that you're driving an avocado green Tercel. Regrettably, madam, the avocado was not the most popular of paint options--wax it and sell it at dusk, that would be my suggestion. "

"Charlie!" The Boss was serious. "Will you, just for a moment, shut the fuck up?"

He startled and shifted his weight to the back of his chair. *Good lord*, he said to himself, *this is one tough broad.* He resolved to adopt the demeanor of a repentant choirboy. Jesus continued,

"Just for the record, Charles, your mother says you were a selfish son, and a cheapskate. The marble headstone was on special. She also says that when you sold her the Ford Malibu, you claimed that all Malibu odometers have a surplus sixth digit and that the 200,000 miles on the clock was really 20,000."

"I said that?" asked Charlie halfheartedly.

"First, you have always belittled the role of women in the making of decisions. You have respected us only in our capacity as cooks and baby factories. In the field of car buying, you have routinely scoffed at us while pretending to assign importance to our opinions."

She had a point, he thought, but most women didn't really mind that much. Did they?

"Second, you have displayed routine racism with respect to Japanese car manufacturers," she shook her head slowly from side to side with an expression of extreme pity, "when, for the last 10 years, Japanese cars have occupied the top 5 spots for car sales in America."

He knew this was true, but always told himself you have to root for your product. You have to knock the competition otherwise what chance do you have?

"Third, you have turned your back on religion. That, Charlie, I take personally."

"Just those three concerns? That's a relief." He tried a big smile. It failed. He went on.

"For a minute, Jesus, I thought there was something serious. Believe me, I understand how you feel, madam. I suppose you're right. I'm not saying you are, but just suppose you are. I...,"

She mimicked a whiny voice "*I can change.*"

"Well? I can."

"Charlie, you had a lifetime to change. Yet every chance you had to hone your boorishness, to work on elevating bigotry to new heights-you took it."

"O.K. Suppose I won't change. Can't change. What then? The subterranean barbecue, I suppose?" Charlie pulled a long face and pointed theatrically at the tunnel behind him.

The image of himself in hell popped up. Being prodded by little red men with pitchforks into a Ford Pinto without air-conditioning, its rear mounted gas rank already ablaze. Personal injury attorneys fawning over him in anticipation. He hung his head.

"There is no barbecue," she said in a kind, soft voice. "Not for you, not for anyone."

"What? Not even for the guy who designed the GMC Pacer?"

"And you *will* change," she went on, "after a spell in Purgatory."

This did not sound good.

"It sounds sinister, Charlie, I know, but you can relax."

She smiled that kind smile again. He felt calmer. "Purgatory has had a bad rap. Just think of it as an on-ramp to Heaven."

Charlie's superior at Paradise Motors was a woman with a fetish for the truth. There was no nationalism in Purgatory - all the cars bore *Made for Heaven* stickers. No matter what options the customer wanted, the car immediately featured them all. Whatever make or model the buyer sought, the desired car appeared in the showroom in front of the customer. Charlie's job was to give the cars away. Free. No sticker price. No retail price. No wholesale price. It was just order taking.

Some weeks later, Jesus crept into the showroom to watch Charlie at work. He was standing in front of a bright red 4x4 with standard options that a young woman had custom ordered a minute earlier.

"I really must go now," the woman was saying.

"Wait up, Susan," she heard Charlie insist. "Are you sure you don't want the air conditioning? The sub-whoofers?"

"No thanks. It's got everything I ordered."

Charlie felt the old urge. "Tell you what, I'll make you a deal, Susan. Here's what I'll do. I'll throw both those options in at no extra cost to you. An unbeatable value, Susan. I'll absorb the overage. My sales manager will kill me. But what the hell, Susan. I like you."

Jesus shook her head, smiling to herself the patient smile of one who knows there are some things that just take time.

Chapter 4

The Suitcase

R ECENTLY JOLTED INTO AWARENESS by job loss and wife departure, Simon is sitting in the kitchen of his San Francisco apartment. It is an October day. He has just turned forty-five.

He stands up and watches the fog swirl through the eucalyptus trees in the park opposite. His life has not amounted to much of anything at all. This is not a dress rehearsal. Maybe Sue Ann was right. Maybe he is "too cautious, too deliberate, too fucking predictable."

Suddenly, Simon makes the decision to become a famous writer. He has always intended to be a writer. It has been the tyranny of the urgent that has kept him from his calling; the domestic chores, building a nest egg, trying to stop Sue Ann from leaving him, feeding the parrot. He has enough money set aside to cover a year's worth of rent and grocery bills and, if it doesn't work out, he can always go back to writing code in darkened rooms for companies he doesn't care about. If it does work out, Sue Ann can read about him in the *New York Times Book Review*.

He buys *The Art of Creative Writing* and highlights in yellow the key passages. *"Be yourself…write what you know… kill your darlings."*

When he has finished, the white sections stand out like snow against an almost continuous yellow background:

Simon decides his *voice* should match his own character: noir with a hint of humor; complicated, but capable of dumbing down to cater to the median intellect.

He applies to Oxford University's Creative Writing Program by means of the most humorous and irony-laden letter. *I will waive my fee in consideration of my desire to enhance the quality of your Program.* The letter accompanies his only finished short story (*The Suitcase*). He changes the date on the yellowed, ten-year-old manuscript and photocopies *The Suitcase* onto fresh paper. He pictures an Oxford professor in a mortarboard and tails opening it with a severe expression, which the academic then struggles to maintain as he reads the entertaining cover letter. Soon the professor's face lights up with wonderment at the sheer skill of the writing.

After a month's silence from Oxford, Simon is forced to attribute their failure to reply to a breakdown in the postal service.

He applies to various writers' programs in the US, focusing on the ones where admission is by selection only. Iowa; Columbia; New York; Rocky Mountain. Time and again. *The Suitcase* jets across country. Simon uses

Express Mail to create a sense of urgency and importance for the recipients. He always strikes out. The responses are vigorous, rapid, and brief.

'Your manuscript does not perfectly mesh with the genre that is our principal focus.' (Iowa)

'We did not see any merit in The Suitcase.' (New York)

He buys a book called *Rejection Letters*. It is a compendium of rejection letters received by famous writers, including Hemingway and Salinger; he feels better.

When his combined Kinko's and Post Office bills exceed $2,000, he settles for a local workshop in Berkeley run by a teacher called Burly Cox with a TV announcer's voice and one minor novel. The workshop contains 20 aspiring writers and takes place in a small craftsman-style cottage at the edge of the campus.

Burly Cox addresses the class. "Good morning. If you haven't read my novel yet, you have missed out on the leading edge of contemporary literature."

Simon surveys the room: a guy with a beret and a scarf who reminds him of a know-it-all he once went to school with.

A beady-eyed schoolmarm type who looks ready to scold anyone who challenges her.

A younger woman in a pink low-cut dress with beckoning body language and the lanky sexuality of a flamingo.

An older man with a satisfied expression on his face like an old lion who has just eaten rather too much wildebeest.

They introduce themselves one by one, each reading a paragraph from their own work. Simon understands quickly that they do not have his talent, but he is touched by their willingness to try to attain the unattainable.

"The suitcase was covered with labels and was brown," he reads when it is his turn, "but it was a dark brown, a sinister brown, reminiscent more of river bottoms than of holidays in the sun." Simon pauses, looks up and scans the room, expecting a "bravo" or perhaps a gasp. What he gets instead is a long silence. Cox coughs and asks the next writer to proceed.

Each week, the writers submit stories to Burly Cox, who reads them out loud anonymously to the group, in a deep, hairy chested Leonard Cohen voice. No one knows who has written a specific story, (except three people), Burly, the story's writer, and Simon (who has secretly shuffled through the pile during the mid-session break).

"In this fashion," Cox tells them, "We ensure constructive criticism that is not personalized."

A pile of stories accumulates on Cox's desk by the beginning of the third class. *The Suitcase* is in there. Cox sorts the stories as though shuffling cards. The group is arranged in chairs in an oval around the living room of the cottage, with Cox at one end of the oval. Simon has taken an aloof seating position on the high-backed armchair opposite Cox at the opposite end of the oval. From this vantage point, he can watch his classmates' expressions and be far enough away from Cox that he can zone out without being noticed if a story is just a waste of good A4.

Flamingo, Beret, Schoolmarm and Lion Face are closer to Cox and are all clearly visible to Simon. As soon as the reading begins, it is obvious to Simon, who prides himself as a maestro in the art of reading body language, who has written each story.

Lion Face's story is, frankly, a study in tedium. So much is left to the reader's imagination, it is an effort to listen to. A death in the first paragraph, a lot of dialogue and some uncomfortable tension between a fighting couple right from the very beginning, but none of the careful descriptions and scene setting that today's reader demands. You end the story without even knowing the color of the protagonist's hair. A common mistake amongst amateurs. At intervals Cox pauses and says things like, "How are we doing so far? Are we rooting for anyone yet? Do we care about the next page?"

"Wonderful hook in line two," Beret says with the look of a gerbil that knows where the nuts are hidden. Simon glances at Cox knowingly, thinking, *what is this, fishing, or writing?*

"Splendid hook, as you say," says Cox.

In a breathy, Marilyn Monroe voice, Flamingo says, "Spare, well-muscled prose that raises the bar with every phrase."

What, are we weightlifting now?

Lion Face basks in the praise. He wears a half smile that says, '*King of the Pride.*'

Flamingo's piece is about nuns. Simon immediately begins doodling in his notebook. No one wants to hear about vespers and ablutions and endless self-denial. The ending is some far-fetched stuff about the key nun running away to be with a lesbian lover, which is as unlikely as it is in poor taste. Anyhow, the readers are never going to believe this kind of thing; something so remote from their daily experience. Write what the reader knows.

Simon's misguided classmates really seem to like it, though. Lion Face speaks of it reverentially as "a fascinating window into a, for most people, alien yet parallel and coexistent universe." This is degenerating into a mutual admiration fest.

Schoolmarm's piece appears to be a vehicle to talk about sex, male body parts and lack of self-restraint. It is called "*The Dress*," and Simon imagines the subtitle 'how many times can I fit the word penis into a short story?' It is clear why Schoolmarm likes an anonymous reading. *The Dress* is too embarrassing even to listen to, let alone have attributed to yourself.

"Brave, brave, piece," says Cox.

"Yes" gushes Flamingo. "Yes, yes, yes. YES!" Simon thinks of the restaurant scene with Meg Ryan and Billy Crystal where the lady at the next table says, "I'll have whatever she's having."

This is beginning to feel more like a therapy session than a writers' group.

"Masterful self-esteem in this piece," says Lion Face. "Self-confidence and the authority to demand the reader's attention."

Go on, ask her for her phone number.

Beret's piece is a monologue. All dialogue with no second character, no descriptive passages, and no relief. Simon is gratified to see that, this time, the reaction is lukewarm, although disappointingly no one calls it "a piece of garbage." Simon sees the tide going against the writer and feels safe wading in.

"Yes, even in my shorter pieces, my sub-novella pieces, I stray away from dialogue. I find that setting the stage through careful, precise, and quite lengthy descriptive sections is vital."

There is an awkward silence, which Cox breaks by calling for the next story.

"*The Suitcase*," he says. "Yes," he coughs, "*The Suitcase*. Indeed."

Simon's heart is thumping, and he struggles to keep a poker expression, but not too hard. If they figure out who wrote it by reading his body language, it will be embarrassing, but pleasantly so.

"Let's read this one straight through," Cox says. "This is the last story, and I want to be sure we have time left at the end for comment."

Simon imagines he is listening to *Short Shorts* on the radio. It is gives him a thrill to hear his own descriptions of the main character, Dick Stern, in Cox's marvelous, deep voice. The meticulous attention to detail, the sunsets in the early days in Florence, the angle of the sunlight falling on

Jane's gingham print dress. The way the name Dick Stern so perfectly matches the sturdy brown suitcase that Dick owns. The shredded stitching in the suitcase's seams. The shape and place names on each of the labels on the Suitcase. The expressions on the faces of the check-in clerks at the airports and the color of the ships' hulls in the harbors. The exact shade of blue of the sunny southern skies at the beginning of the piece, fading artfully as Dick's hopes fade to the quality of darkness in the clouds of the later northern destinations. The thundershowers at the end in Iceland, foreshadowing Dick's despair as Jane tells him she cannot bear to be with him anymore. The marvelous symbolism of the final paragraph, where the Suitcase slides along the conveyor belt, alone and homeward bound, with Jane's baggage speeding by in the opposite direction. When the story is finished, Simon can feel himself blush. He glances around and catches the Flamingo looking at him. He has the impression that she may have figured out who wrote it. He is gratified by the group's thoughtful, appreciative silence.

For a while.

No one speaks. He looks up and wonders if anyone else has figured out he is the author. As the silence continues, he begins to hope not. Eventually Cox intervenes. "What do you think of *The Suitcase*?"

Beret says, "It is a story about a suitcase, but it is really about Dick. The suitcase never does anything unexpected. Neither does Dick. It is too predictable. There is no dialogue at all. Can they speak? Perhaps they are mutes?"

Simon feels the blow deep in his insides.

"It's kind of boy meets girl, boy bores girl, boy loses girl?" Cox says.

Lion Face joins the fray. "The story is a bore because the story takes no risks. Dick and his suitcase take no risks. Furthermore," he says pompously, "we do not get inside their heads. We know what Dick looks like, kind of like his suitcase, but we do not know what he *feels* like."

"In other words, we really don't care much about Dick, because we don't know much about him?" Cox asks.

"Well, we know one thing for sure," Schoolmarm says, "from line one we know Dick is going to lose the girl. He's such a damn bore. Trailing her off to Italy and Finland and every point of the compass in between, but they never actually do anything. As far as we know, they never even have sex. I mean the lady wanted a good time. Dick might as well have stayed home with Jane and watched the National Geographic Channel. They could have saved a lot of money if they'd left the damned suitcase in the attic where it belonged."

Simon has moved from indignation right through rage and into emotional pain. His eyes well with tears and he fights them off.

Composing himself, he says, "Maybe Dick's happy with his life. Perhaps Jane was ungrateful and unappreciative of all the lovely places he took her. Maybe he's better off without her."

Flamingo looks at Cox. The heat in the cottage has made her face flush. In profile she is looking spectacularly sensual. "Dick is a dodo," she says. "He just lays back and accepts the inevitable without a fight, like, why bother? But if someone got to him, maybe he could change enough, within the story, to come out ahead. I think that's believable. I think the story is crying out for Dick to grow a pair and run after Jane like Hoffman in the Graduate. He needs to beat on her doors and change her mind."

Flamingo looks straight at Simon, and he holds her gaze. She really is quite beautiful.

Then she turns back toward Cox, giggling slightly. "Oops, silly. There I go writing someone's ending for them again."

Chapter 5

Two Left Feet and a Motorcycle

IT WAS 1997. EARLY summer.

Smog hung heavy over Los Angeles, and humidity enveloped us like a comforter we were too tired to throw off. Things between me and Crystal weren't good. Crystal loved to entertain. She liked the sound of laughter in a crowded room, and old-fashioned ballroom dancing at Balloons dance hall. I liked peace and quiet. Motorcycling on the coast road. Reading a good book for hours in the bathroom.

In the early days, we both pretended to like things we didn't. Crystal would ride pillion on my Triumph through the dawn ocean mist. Lately, she always had an excuse. Now I didn't dare start the bike, idle so long that mice had built a nest in the tailpipes. Besides, it would have been unkind to wake them. The thing now was that Crystal no longer pretended.

I was a terrible dancer, but I was still doing my best. I took lessons on my own to mitigate my public displays of ineptitude. I really tried to like it. I still loved how Crystal sparkled and shone. I tried as hard as I could to keep up. Even so, my two worst nightmares were the Tango and dancing with anyone but Crystal.

She called me at work one Friday morning. "Halcyon's tonight?" Halcyon's was the new *ballroom revival* place on the West Side. "Lucy and Dick will be there".

I had resolved to agree with everything Crystal wanted. I was scared of losing her.

"Sure."

"You don't sound thrilled exactly."

"No. Really. I am."

I wasn't.

Lucy was Crystal's best friend. A magnificent woman whom I strove to impress. She was five eleven and large, with a full bosom, which her height allowed her to carry off. She had smiling eyes that said, "You are really something". Many times, Lucy had offered to be there for me if anything should happen to Crystal. She had no pretensions. She hated her husband, Dick, because he was a dick; he had cheated on her. Crystal said Lucy wouldn't leave him because she was a big softy who felt sorry for him.

At Halcyon's, awkward in my tuxedo and baking under the hot yellow lights, I felt like a penguin at the equator. I danced a few dances with Crystal. She hardly looked at me, and the more inadequate I felt, the worse my timing got. When I clasped her hand, mine was sweaty, and hers was dry and cool. I tried hard to follow her lead but halfway through the third dance, a fox-trot, her arms went limp, and she gave me a *what's the use?* glare and walked over to the bar. Standing alone on the parquet, under the hot bright lights, I knew that would be our last dance that night.

While Dick was dancing with Crystal, Lucy came up behind me and put her hand on my shoulder. I must have cringed because she said, "Don't worry. I won't ask you to dance."

I felt myself relax. "Two left feet," I apologized.

"You're a good man, Charlie Brown, and don't you forget it." I could tell she meant it.

One Sunday a month later, Crystal and I were in the kitchen of our condo when she asked me to move out. There was no big scene. I stared out over the haze of Pasadena. The freeways were at a standstill, and I couldn't see the mountains. It was 9:00 am, and I was already sweating.

"Sam, you're capable of anything. You have a big heart. You're handsome. Funny when you want to be."

When she talked like this, there was always a 'but'.

"But you're not sociable. You are very sweet to pretend to like my friends, the dancing. But it's not you."

I licked the salt off my lips. Sweat, not a tear.

"I just can't wait around any longer to watch the butterfly emerge from the chrysalis."

I was crushed. I blamed it on the dancing and my weak chin. Two weeks later, I moved into the second floor of a decrepit Victorian in the wrong neighborhood. The landlady, Mrs. Steinhertz, lived on the ground floor. Clothes-moths the size of pterodactyls flapped about in my closet. To distract me from the loneliness, I had just made the decision to bury myself in work. That was when I got a call from H.R. that they were laying me off.

Cash low, too much thinking time on my hands, I started drinking cheap wine and moping about. There was clearly no hope for me, no future. I was a loser. Some nights I just sat in my bedroom listening to the drone of Mrs. Steinhertz's TV through the floorboards, and the beating of moth wings against the closet doors. I endured my loneliness until mid-December. Then, when I was in Macys one night looking for a robust shirt that could survive the carnage in Mrs. Steinhart's closet, the urge to find love again suddenly overwhelmed me. A soft-faced woman was holding up a man's sweater, bright red with a pattern of big snowflakes on it. She held it out to the light. I knew she was picturing her husband or lover in it. Suddenly, desperately, I wanted to be *wearing that sweater.* As I headed for home through the mall's parking lot in the rain, couples and families were trussing trees onto their roof racks and racing home to decorate them. I stood by my car and took in the scene. Memory has embellished it in my mind, but it felt something like this:

All the children had laughter in their eyes. Parents standing beside SUV's held hands like first time lovers. The children rolled down the rear windows as the cars drove out of the lot in convoy, and from every back seat came the sweet sound of children singing *Silent Night.* I stood motionless as the line of cars grew, and with every chorus, the deeper voices of the parents broke in and swelled until the air was full of Christmas.

I needed a drink.

I got home and poured a tumbler of Bulgarian wine, with a label stating something like: *Warning. 100% sulfites. Call ambulance prior to removing cap.* There were ten Christmas cards on the TV, nine of which had been forwarded from work-from clients who didn't know I had lost my job-and my wife. The tenth was from my mother. *Happy Christmas Sammy. Next time, let me meet her before you marry her. Mom.* I glanced at the dusty mirror on the wall. Clearly, my teeth had lost their youthful luster, and my hair had receded like the tree line in a forest fire. I grabbed a handful on top of my head and pulled. One, two three...eleven. Eleven hairs. Just as I thought. I would be bald as a plucked turkey by next summer. I left the lights off in the gathering gloom and sat in the living room facing the hypothetical spot where Crystal and I might have put the tree if we had still been together and lived in this flat. Job hunting at Christmas was pretty discouraging. I called the ad agency where I had applied the previous week for a low-level administrative position. A woman with the personality of a snapping turtle told me.

"We will not address personnel issues until the New Year."

What she really meant was *"Go away, you pathetic person. I am wrapped in the Christmas glow of loving and giving."* (But mainly receiving). *"Don't invade my bubble with your neediness. How did you get into this hopeless state anyhow? Jobless at Christmas?"* At least now I could concentrate full time on hunting for a love life. I talked to myself in cliches to psyche myself up. "Nothing ventured", "carpe diem", "just do it". Warmed by the sulfites, I began to see myself as a man who brushes off defeats like dandruff from a shoulder. I had a good singing voice. I could write love stories. I would make a wonderful father. There had been three women in my life who had liked me enough to sleep with me. Jack Nicholson's hair was thinning, and he still maintained an active love life. Back then, online dating was still fifteen years away. We used personal ads in the newspapers. I wrote mine the next morning and mailed it to the paper from the mailbox at the end of the street before I could change my mind.

Santa seeking Santette.
Honest divorced man, 40, wants mate. Must be female.
Warning: Two left feet and a motorcycle.

The next day, I was appalled at what I had done. With the morning light came the usual feelings of self-loathing and inadequacy. The bravado of the night before had vanished. Women would not be interested in a man with no job, dwindling follicles and two left feet. There were hundreds of eligible men out there. Suave, handsome conversationalists with teeth like piano keys, mortgage-free homes, and hair that resembled lions' manes. It was, however, too late. Back then, the routine was that the newspaper assigned you an anonymous voice mailbox. A computerized voice would say *please leave a message,* and women answering the ad would leave messages. If you liked what you heard, you called them back. I drew a bath and settled into the hot water. I listened to the first one. A gentle female voice spoke sweetly to me.

"This is Sandy. I'm 36, five nine. People tell me I am *very* attractive. *Loved* your ad." She went on to tell me why she had broken up with her boyfriend, where she was born, and that she was quite shy about physical intimacy but warmed up once she got to know you better.

I saved the message. There was another. And another. By the time I had listened to them all that first night, fourteen women had phoned me and told me things that even their mothers didn't know. I felt sad that so many felt they needed to stress their physical attributes, as if they had been told that's all men were interested in. I wanted to interrupt them mid-message and reassure them that, at least for me, that was not it at all.

Every one of these women was apparently beautiful. They wanted not just to meet me, but to spend the rest of their lives with me. I reread my ad and congratulated myself. *Santette.* The cleverness of it all. No wonder I was so sought after. I scanned the other ads and recognized at once how corny they all were by comparison. I began to feel sorry for the lonely, uncreative men who had placed them, sitting alone, hearing *your mailbox is empty.* A glow of magnanimity came over me and I had the urge to forward some of my messages to my suffering, less creative brethren.

Picky thoughts came into my head. Would my mother like them? How could I be guaranteed they didn't like to dance? Really liked motorcycles? Wanted children?

I developed a new routine. I would wander around town during the day, and in the evenings, I would listen to the messages in the bath. I went to bed happy every night. By the third night, I had forty-seven messages from women who adored me. I had had one glass too many of *Select Reserve* Bulgarian wine and the screenwriter in me toyed with a ludicrous parody of male chauvinism. I would rent a gymnasium and invite the callers to a pageant-style interview. They would come in cheerleaders' outfits, with ribbons across their chests stating their best characteristics, gleaned from the messages they had left in the mailbox.

Heart of gold.
Loves animals.
Don't make me dance.

A panel of judges (a mixture of celebrities and marriage counselors, including the then legendary sex therapist, Doctor Ruth), would whittle down the crowd to a final three, who would answer prepared questions from cards.

Why do you think you deserve Sam Christian?

How does Sam know you will ride pillion on his motorcycles after you have stopped trying to impress him?

How will you adapt to being the breadwinner?

The final three contestants would parade in a variety of themed outfits.

On the Triumph; meeting Sam's mother; Valentine's Night; Pregnant mother.

Finally, a police expert would do age-adjusted sketches of each of the candidates, projected to age 45, 50, 60 and 70.

I would make the final pick after conferring with the judges. The winner would live with me on a year's trial, and if I was not satisfied, I could move on to number two, then number three, and so on. I was aware even then how unsavory this frame of mind was, but it was cozy and risk free, gorging on messages. I was in denial that I knew I would eventually actually have to return some calls. On day four, I listened to a last batch and psyched myself up. One message came from a familiar voice. Out of its context, it took me a few seconds to place. Lucy.

"I love to dance, I should warn you, but I can deal with two left feet. I have two right ones. And anyone is trainable. Call me."

I forgot the other messages, forgot everything. Just to hear a familiar voice, especially Lucy's, was enough to get my pulse racing. I called her on the number she had left, which was her home number. I already had it anyway. She had no idea I had heard her message on the voicemail. I just said I was checking in, now that I was on my own, and looking to hear a familiar voice. A lie of omission, I knew, but a white lie. No harm intended or done.

Dick had done it again. This time he was history.

I was glowing.

"If he had just gone and done it," Lucy said, "then I *might* have been able to handle it. Maybe. Maybe not. But then he tried to con me with a half dozen alibis about where he was that night and how he respected me too much to sleep around. Horseshit. If you are going to sleep around, you tell your mate and give them the choice. Stay or go."

"You deserved better." I said, self-servingly.

We talked for a long time. We made a date.

"Sammy, you looked so dapper in that tuxedo," she said. "Just for fun, let's dress up in our dance outfits and look into Bubbles for old times' sake. Then dinner."

"No dancing." I said.

"I won't make you dance." she said."

"OK," I said. "It's a deal."

By the time we hung up, the bath water was cold.

Inside Bubbles, my palms immediately began to sweat. Lucy dove in, but I hung back. I was terrified. I felt a hundred eyes on me. *There's the dork who can't dance. Taking up valuable real estate.* Lounge lizards in tuxedos swept effortlessly about the brightly lit room, as if on wheels. Their legs never actually touched the ground. *Masterful* was the word that sprang to mind. The lizards' partners, all big hair and rustling crinoline, wore fixed expressions of rapture, as though mid-way through the perfect orgasm. I looked down to where a dime sized moth hole graced my lapel.

I felt Lucy's hand on my shoulder.

"Nervous, handsome? Come on, join the party!"

"No way Lucy! We had a deal."

"I lied about no dancing."

Lucy was wearing her favorite bright orange low cut dancing gown. My inadequacy gripped me. I froze up. She took a hold of me and hugged me as if we were a war bride and a P.O.W. reuniting at a train station.

The band launched into a tango. Lucy had a wonderful sense of the beat and could move gracefully, despite her size. Her hand was as sweaty as mine. I tried to pull free, but she began strutting like a lyre bird with orange plumage, whipping me around and then pulling me back towards her. I felt like a black and white horizontal yo-yo. She was dancing the male steps, and I the female. Somehow, suddenly, it didn't matter. It was fun. Her rhythm flowed into me. I was sweating and smiling, and she was laughing and strutting. As soon as I relaxed and stopped trying, I became the best dancer in the world. Everything was a tangerine blur. I raised my head every fourth step to gasp for breath, like a freestyle swimmer, then plunged back into the heaven of her cleavage. Suddenly, greased by sweat, our hands parted, and I flew away from her as if off a centrifuge and landed in the middle of the floor.

As she bent over to pick me up, I noticed something in her eyes, felt it in my own.

Just a hint, but it was there, for sure.

"Two left feet? It was your ad I answered, wasn't it?" She smiled.

"Yes."

The next dance was slow, and as I held her, I could smell the perspiration on the softness of her neck, and it reminded me of a happy time, long before dancing lessons.

PART TWO

SHOCK AND AWE

MEN IN LOVE

Chapter 6

Magic

I thought magic

Was just a party trick

Until I fell in love.

Chapter 7

Wingy Sleeves

You glide into my world and land here,

a black swan that cannot exist

but does.

You are the hummingbird flying backwards towards me

from a long-abandoned nest of dreams

dripping nectar into my open mouth

as you come.

You are all winged creatures,

brushing my face with almost-imagined wing tips,

inviting these eyes skyward to watch,

through a film of tears of disbelief as you soar.

Chapter 8

Scent

Emily and Jason are in bed. Jason feels the heat from the fire flickering in the hearth as the winter storm dumps snow on the moors outside.

Hector watches them both out of one eye from his perch at the foot of the bed. African Grey parrots are supposed to be even smarter than dolphins. Hector often warns Jason of thunder and unexpected visitors. It makes Jason feel safe to have him around.

Emily is lying on her stomach, looking directly into Jason's eyes. She has propped herself up on her elbows with her face cupped in her hands.

"I love you, you know, Jason. You big, manly, but not too hairy man." Jason leans towards her. She goes on.

"You Argonaut. You sensitive, but not too sensitive man of my dreams. You man with callused hands yet a touch so light that my nipples sit up and think they must have imagined it."

"When you talk like that, Em, you can alter whole weather patterns." Jason leans further forward.

"And the weather forecast for the bedroom is for high pressure, followed by heavy showers and a big wet spot."

They laugh together. Emily opens her mouth to catch her breath, and he kisses it hard and slides under her. She slips off her t-shirt, looking down at him, her pale green eyes smiling. Jason inhales her scent and puts on a show for her, making like a wine taster savoring a merlot.

To Jason, Emily's scent in bed is woman and girl and safety and home-at-last and permanence. It is strength and softness and stubbornness. It is a scent he seems to have known forever.

"Call the cops!" shouts Hector. They are beyond laughing now. They ignore the bird.

Afterwards, maneuvering them both into dry territory and switching the light back on, Jason hugs Emily's back and tucks his knees under hers. Her body radiates its familiar heat. She always feels ten degrees hotter than he does. "Real women don't spoon," Emily says sleepily.

"But real men do," Jason says. "Anyway, spooning is a condition of our union."

Emily sighs. "Okay then. Safe to morning. Love you big boy."

"Love you too."

Jason studies the short hair on the back of Emily's neck as her breathing deepens into sleep. Always being this close in bed; always sleeping with the light on; these are issues that Emily accepted up front. She made Jason feel that his twin demons, darkness and being alone, didn't make him less of a man.

She told him up front, "Jason. Your reasons are actual reasons. Most men would be in the loony bin after what you've been put through. Let me see now; deranged babysitter banishes seven year old Jason to bedroom as darkness falls. Frightened boy comes out of room already scared shitless and tiptoes upstairs in darkness. Boy wonders why babysitter is silent. Boy searches every room. Boy finds babysitter hanging by neck from jump rope attached to light fixture in kitchen. Parents don't get home for another two hours. Case closed, for God's sake."

This is the first time in his adult life that Jason remembers feeling safe. The depression and suicidal thoughts of the past seem to be part of someone else's life now. Emily's cottage outside Exeter is in the heart of the Devon countryside. He sees an extraordinary beauty in the flatness and desolation of the vast heathland. The window in the study where he writes his screenplays looks out across Dartmoor, where the mythical Hound of the Baskervilles once prowled its hollows at the dead of night.

By day, the remoteness does not bother him; it inspires him and helps him concentrate. The main distraction is Hector's constant banter.

"Where's Emily? Where's Emily?" and "Writer's block. Writer's block."

But by night it is a different matter. The remoteness really does bother him except that Emily has always kept her word never to be home more than an hour or two after dark. Her job in London is just a two-hour train ride away. The routine's the same every night. Emily's train pulls into Exeter station at six thirteen. She gets her car from the parking lot and drives home; she walks through the cottage door at around seven, to the sound of Hector's "Here's Emily. Here's Emily." As he closes his eyes, Jason thinks of how sacred, how essential this routine has become to him.

When Jason awakens the next day, Emily has long gone, as usual. He smiles; she never misses the train. Her wristwatch is her conscience. Through the window he can only just make out her faint tire tracks, almost covered by newly fallen snow.

"Get up lazy boy. Feed Hector. Feed Hector. Feed Hector. Feed Hector. Lazy boy."

It is a day for rewriting a difficult section of script. Jason finds his attention wandering to the heavy snowfall outside, and the long wait for Emily's return.

Just after five, like always, Jason carries Hector on his index finger into the sitting room and turns on the big TV to catch the news. The huge bright screen and Hector's company always help him ignore the darkness demons until Emily gets home.

Tonight, though, Jason cannot settle. There is no captivating news, and after a few minutes Hector startles him by flapping his wings in sharp bursts and squawking noisily, as though trying to say something for which he does not have the words. Jason tries everything, but the bird will not settle. Finally, Jason calms him with a hunk of cuttlebone.

The jingle that introduces the six o'clock news sounds from the television set.

The newscaster's voice comes on,

"Breaking news. This just in. Shortly after five o'clock this evening, the main line evening commuter train from London to Exeter derailed outside Taunton on frozen points in a blizzard. The train plunged down an Embankment and into the river Wye. First reports suggest that no survivors are likely."

Jason's mind immediately fills with dread; anger; fear; denial. His mind has nowhere to go; no place to take him. The phone rings and for a moment he does not recognize the sound over the blare of the TV.

Hector screams, "Get the phone. Get the phone. Get the phone."

Mechanically, Jason picks up the phone and Emily's breathless voice at the other end says, "Sweetheart? You've seen it, haven't you? I just heard it on the radio. I'm driving. I borrowed a car from Mary at work. I missed the train. The staff meeting ran over. Don't be afraid. It's me. Jason? Jason? Speak to me."

"I...can't. I'm so ... It's ...."

Jason's legs feel tired and unsteady. He squats down on his haunches and steadies himself with one hand on the carpet. Emily's voice comes through again. "Look, I'll be there by eight. Drink a scotch. Get Hector talking. Change the channel. Phone your mum."

He feels himself calming, light-headed almost.

"Emily. Can you... stay on the line?"

"Of course, darling. "

"No. I mean all the way down; until you get here?"

"Of course, sweetheart. What shall we talk about?"

"Last night."

"The great flood?"

"Right."

"Okay. Let's get Noah on the conference line."

"Unless he's busy with all those animals. I wonder if he has a wife for Hector?"

And they talk and listen and fall silent and talk again. Jason overdoes the Glenlivet. They lose reception a few times. Suddenly, headlights sweep up the driveway and Emily trudges up to the door. Jason can see her breath making clouds against the darkness. Snowflakes fall from her coat onto the porch, and she steps inside.

As they hug in the living room, relief comes to Jason like sunshine on the Dales. Emily's hair has a musty smell that seems somehow out of place, but scotch and the joy of having her home safe push it into the background.

Jason carries Hector back to the perch in the bedroom. Emily goes to the bathroom and then they watch a corny romance together in bed. Jason holds Emily's hand on his chest. Hector fluffs his feathers and grooms frantically.

"Where's Emily? Where's Emily?" Usually this is his calm time. It has been a strange day.

In the bathroom, Jason glances at Emily's watch where she has taken it off by the sink. It says 5:13. Not like Emily, but it has been a strange day.

Back in bed, Emily already has her clothes off and her back toward him. She must be exhausted. Jason settles in behind her in the spoon position and holds her hard and firm. She feels very cold, as though she has carried the night into the cottage with her.

"Real women don't spoon, you know," Emily says, dreamily, "I'll make an exception tonight though. And every night. I'll love you always, big boy." Her voice sounds as if it is far away. Too much scotch.

"Ditto," says Jason. He buries his head in the back of Emily's hair and inhales, seeking the comfort of her scent. He breathes in again, confused. There is something out of place. He recognizes it. What he smells is not Emily, after all. It is the smell of a crowded railway carriage where the cigarette smoke sticks to the cloth seats.

Jason releases his grip and moves away.

Hector squawks frantically.

"Where's Emily? Where's Emily? Where's Emily?"

Chapter 9

You Never Know When

This could be the last time, I don't know - The Rolling Stones

My Daughter

WHEN MY DAUGHTER WAS little, I read her a bedtime story every night. Many nights I got home late, and she waited up for me. Sometimes I would feel her little hands pulling at my arm, saying, "Daddy! You're sleeping!" and I would try to pretend I was just resting my eyes. It never fooled her. The books changed as the years passed. Our first book was *Pat the Bunny*, where she patted the furry tummy of a rabbit that popped out of its pages. Then we graduated to *How Much Do I Love You?* where she competed with me to raise our arms to the sky saying, "So high!" and then "To the infinity sky," and then, "Beyond infinity," until she fell asleep.

There was *Goodnight Moon*, and *Winnie The Pooh* and *Peter Rabbit* and *Where The Wild Things Are*. A year or so after that we read *Madeline's Adventures in Paris*, and then she fell in love with Mufasa in the *Lion King*. We sang "Akuna Matata" together, the warthog's "don't worry" song. Much later, she fell in love with horses, and could read, so we took it in turns to read alternate pages of *My Friend Flicka*, and *Black Beauty*.

When she got to nine or ten, we read *The Red Pony* by Steinbeck (a bit of a leap by me). The title held the promise of a young girl grooming a pony, and riding it across the open prairies of the wild west, reveling in the thrill and the freedom. In the first five pages, the pony died a slow and horrible death at the hands of a disease called strangles, which is exactly what it sounds like. We laughed about it for weeks afterwards and she nicknamed Steinbeck's masterpiece *The Dead Pony*.

But by far her favorite was *Racing Stripes*, about a baby zebra who is rescued from a traveling circus by Nolan, a racehorse trainer. Stripes the zebra lives on Nolan's farm with Channing his 13-year-old daughter. Stripes dreams of competing in races, unaware that he is in fact a zebra. He is mocked and bullied by the local thoroughbred, Trenton's Thunder. Stripes and Channing enter the 'Kentucky Open', but their rivals try to sabotage them. Channing remembers Nolan's advice, *Don't look back. Leave it all on the track.* Channing and Stripes win the race, beating the race favorite Trenton's Thunder, in a photo finish.

One of our very last stories was a book called *Coraline*, in which the girl steps through a hidden door to find another house strangely similar to her own (only better). She is thrilled. But there is another mother there, and another father, who want her to stay and be their little girl. They kidnap her and try to change her and never let her go. Coraline has to fight with all her courage to escape this living hell and return to her ordinary life. I still have PTSD from it, so goodness knows how my daughter feels. She is thirty now.

I don't recall which the last book we read was, but there must have been one, just as there must have been one night that was the last time I ever read her a bedtime story. I never knew it would be the last time.

But it was.

My Dad

My dad fought the Nazis in a tank in the Second World War. He never talked about it, but he must have been frightened every hour of every day. Recently, I was sorting through some old dusty boxes in the attic and found a yellowed war department report book labeled *secret* which showed detailed accounts of all the battles. In one of them, his tank had been cornered by ten of Hitler's newest inventions, the Panzer tank. It was, literally, unstoppable. Nothing could disable it, no shell, no explosion, no mine, and no grenade. Twenty-seven of the thirty tanks in my dad's regiment never made it out.

Growing up in London, the father I knew was reserved, but when it was just our family together at home, he could be incredibly funny. He was a truly kind man. He would bring all four of us children a cup of tea at seven every morning. I don't think he ever missed a day.

I often think of Robert Hayden's poem.

> Sundays too. My father got up early
>
> and put his clothes on in the blue-black cold,
>
> then with cracked hands that ached
>
> from labor in the weekday weather
>
> he made banked fires blaze.
>
> What did I know then, what did I know
>
> of love's austere and lonely offices?

By the time I was eighteen, he had retired and with no routine or purpose to his existence, drinking had disabled him. One day he surprised me by giving me five hundred pounds to buy my first car, a well-used Volkswagen beetle. It was old, but it was reliable. I loved looking out of my bedroom window on cold November days in England and seeing its cheery orange paintwork.

Dad was a member of the Naval and Military Club near Green Park, a posh area of London. One Saturday afternoon in July when I was home from University, I heard him stumbling up the stairs in our big house. I went into the kitchen to greet him. Dangling from a hook in the larder were two pheasants, feathers intact, that a friend of his had given him. In those days, shooting was a big pastime for some people, although my dad did not take part himself. He did not enjoy shooting at all.

I said, "Good morning, Dad," as he teetered towards the larder and unhooked the two birds.

"I'm going to the club," he said, slurring his words. "Dickie is partial to pheasant. I am going to give him this brace." (A pair of pheasant was known as a *brace* back then.)

"Dad," I said, "It is best if you wait till tomorrow. Dickie will not be there—it's Saturday."

He ignored me and headed to the front door, fumbling with the latch as he tried to open it.

"Dad!" I lost my temper. "You are NOT going. Wait 'til tomorrow!" I knew he was going to take the train to our little country cottage in Friston the next day, and my mother could cook the birds while he was away.

"Goodbye," he slurred. "I will catch the 33."—the bus that would take him to the Club.

I grabbed the door handle with one hand and the pheasants with the other, and stood between him and the door. "No!" I shouted, "Wait 'til tomorrow." I could smell the whisky on his breath.

He tried to get around me, and something in me thought, *let him go. If he is going to make a fool of himself, it is not my job to stop him.*

I moved aside and opened the door. He stumbled down the front steps, almost falling as he did so. Then he headed the half mile down Kensington Church Street, the steep hill that led to the bus stop. I sat in a chair in the drawing room, stewing over my outburst. The guilt overtook me. What kind of son would ditch his father like that? I grabbed my car keys and hurried out of the house to the beetle. I caught up with him a couple of minutes later, staggering down the sidewalk, sweating in the hot sun, and clutching the string that held the pheasants. I opened the VW's passenger door, and he practically fell into the seat. I drove him to his club and dropped him off. I helped him up the steps and asked the doorman to take care of him. The man gave me a knowing look.

"Goodbye dad," I said. "I bet Dickie will love the pheasants. Promise you will phone me if you need a lift home." Late that evening, he arrived back home. The doorman must have hailed a taxi for him.

The next morning, I woke up late. He was gone. There was a piece of lined paper on the hall table, and on it there was a note in his neat handwriting written in pencil. I still have that note fifty years later. 'Have *departed* to Friston.' Nobody used that word anymore. Today we would say *gone*.

Three days later I got a call from a friend of his in Friston. Dad's heart had given out. He was dead. He was sixty-four.

I could not have known this was the last time I would ever see him.

But it was.

My Surprise

The third of my disastrous marriages had just ended. I can't cope with cheating. I believe there is an 'off switch', that once you have given up your belief that love or trust exist with a partner, it is irreversible. No amount of therapy and determination can rescue the feeling you once had. I think that the only thing worse than being alone, is being alone, but together. I had given up on love. I began to think that if you have never had a partner you can trust, you never will. No point in hoping.

One day I was asked to attend a work function in Toronto. I decided not to go. I lived near San Francisco, and had lost my passport, so I knew I would be turned back at the Canadian border. I had a colleague in Seattle who was due to make a presentation at the same conference, but couldn't attend. She had a bad cold and couldn't fly. But her boss was a very demanding man, and told her she had no choice; he needed her to make the presentation, and she should just "get over it."

I ran a large part of the company, and as the date approached, I began to get heavy pressure from the company's President to go. A few days before the event, I decided I would risk it. My strategy was to fly to Blaine, Washington, a few miles from the Canadian border, and rent a car. I would drive through the border, looking as innocent as I knew how, and hope the border guards would not stop me. They did not.

My colleague responded to the demands from her boss and decided she had no choice but to go. She suffered through the misery of flying with congestion and pressure changes on the plane, and arrived at the hotel the day before the event.

There was a company dinner with a celebrity guest, and about a hundred attendees. We were all to be seated at a series of long tables; I searched for a seat, but there was a scrimmage with everyone trying to get the choicest location. My Seattle colleague glided gracefully towards one of only two open seats. Like Moses parting the Red Sea, the crowd cleared a pathway to allow her to sit down. I saw the remaining opening, and like a competition for a parking spot, a large man tried to take the seat I was about to sit in. I swung my butt towards him and pressed forcefully into his ample bottom, parking my own rear firmly in the spot.

As the evening wore on, dinner was served, and speeches were made. She and I began small talk about work and other standard topics. Although we had worked at the same company for ten years, we didn't really know much about each other. As the evening progressed, I found myself revealing personal nuggets, such as how I was a writer and a Londoner and a fan of the Rolling Stones. She was more reticent, and I got the impression that she was not comfortable talking about her personal life with work colleagues. Wine flowed, and we found ourselves facing each other, with our backs to the people on either side. Slowly, like a Russian nesting doll, she shed her outer layers and began telling me about herself. She, too, was a writer and a fan of Mick Jagger. She was a student of British Royalty and talked of visiting Buckingham Palace and the Tower of London.

I noticed for the first time her sparkling green eyes, one obscured be a fringe of silky blond hair. It gave me the same feeling I had as a fifteen-year-old at the height of my love affair with Twiggy, the British model in the poster I had pinned to my bedroom wall.

You see, we had no choice. It was love at first sight–the myth that is not a myth.

We are married now, and here we are, the magic just as fresh as it was all those years ago in Toronto.

Before that evening, I never knew I would fall in love. Truly, you never know when.

But I did.

Chapter 10

String Theory

You died last night, at ten nineteen p.m.

They wheeled you out.

And that's a fact.

Great minds try to crack the cypher to

the contents of the book of us,

the volume without numbers on its pages,

the book that shrugs aside the bookends on the tiny shelf of

now.

The scientists look beyond the farthest edges

of the distant constellations

and yet the truth defies their calculations

and is impervious to the probings of their minds designed to

solve.

The inexplicable have surrendered.

String Theory

Dark Matter

Higgs Bosun

The Missing Bayons of the Universe

The Time-Space Continuum spits out facts

but gags on magic.

You died last night, at ten nineteen p.m.

They wheeled you out.

And that's a fact.

But you are here beside me,

and we're chatting,

although it's three a.m.

And that's a fact.

Chapter 11

Something Lost

I AM LYING IN bed, looking out at the lawn through the French windows. Sarah designed it to be an outside-inside house. She wanted to see Josh playing in the garden from every room.

Her side of the bed was closest to the window, before she opted out. Some mornings I couldn't tell, from watching her back, whether she was sleeping or gazing out towards Josh's turtle-shaped sandbox perched at the far end of the lawn, where the ground rises slightly before it reaches the back fence. The sandbox was filled with brightly colored dump trucks and tractors.

I miss the engine noises Josh used to make in the sandbox. I wonder if he'll ever want to play again.

Through the trees that border the rear fence, there is a clear sky and just a hint of the morning sun. It must be about seven o'clock.

Josh is searching the house. He does this most days. Looks for her. I can hear him above my head in the kitchen, then the living room, then on the front porch and back in again. His feet come down the stairs, past his bedroom and down the hall to where I am. I sit up in bed.

He pads into the room, staring straight ahead, his diaper sticking out from his behind like a billowed spinnaker. He goes to the window and gazes out toward the sandbox. Then he turns back around, goes to Sarah's side of the bed, and pulls himself up on tippy toes to stare at the spot she used to occupy. For me, this was the place where we would make love in the years before it happened. The place where later she slept in short frantic bursts; the place from which she first spoke to me late into the night of her fears and her sadness and the private devils that were eventually to claim her.

For Josh, Sarah's side was a different place. This was mom's side, where she breastfed him; where she soothed away fevers and bad dreams and held him close against the storms.

Josh slides back down to the floor and comes around to my side of the bed. He holds his little arms out for me to gather him and I pull him up onto my lap. He leans away and studies my face with his light brown eyes. A serious expression, chasing down the truth from under his blond bangs. I can tell he is about to ask a question, and I am preparing for how I will answer, the strength I have to show him and the comforting I must give when I cannot comfort myself.

"Dad, I was wondering. Have you seen my yellow tractor?" His little arm points at the window.

"You know, dad, the yellow one."

Chapter 12

Kite

You are a kite in the wind

not an aeroplane

You are a heartbeat

not a pump.

You are a river

not a canal.

You are a sea

not a reservoir.

You are driftwood

not a canoe.

You do not plan

you take what comes.

You do not choose

life chooses you.

You are a wildfire

not a controlled burn.

You love what comes your way

not what you chase.

Chapter 13

Detours

The acrid final smell of final bridges burning, the sudden green to brown of fall leaves turning, the bridle foam that capped the white waves churning. These unplanned detours ridiculed the careful route I planned.

And every day felt like a winter Monday. The colors in my world were simply gray.

The spinning of the compass had me reeling, and wounds from former conflicts were past healing, when, from the sky your feathered soul came wheeling, on sinewed wings and plucked me from that unforgiving land.

So Monday's mourner has turned Sunday's bridegroom,

now scent of you has found a friendly breeze and blown my

way.

Chapter 14

Angelface

IT WAS EARLY ONE evening in January and already dark outside, when the phone rang. Emily was drawing carefully in crayon on a big pad of paper in the middle of the kitchen floor. It was a picture for her second-grade class project, *Our Parents at Work*. At the top, she had printed the words MY MOM AT BALLET CLASS. She was propped on one elbow, her tiny pink ballet slippers tucked up behind her miniature bottom. Her blonde hair was in a pony tail, gathered up in a red velvet ribbon. She had drawn Sarah on tiptoes, grasping the leather rail in front of the mirror, facing her class with her arm arched above her head. Emily was struggling with drawing the mirror image, which would not come out exactly like the image it reflected. She liked things to be exact, certain. I remembered later that the picture gave the impression that Sarah was leaning on the rail rather heavily, for support, and the rail was bowing down where her hand rested.

Sarah and I were sitting without speaking at the kitchen table, avoiding each other's glances. I had been dreading the call. We had agreed that if it was bad news, we would not let on to Emily. There would be time later to explain about red cells and white cells. The phone rang. Sarah and I both jumped across the kitchen to grab for it. Sarah won. I moved very close to her so that my nose was touching her auburn hair, and rested my hand on her slender, white forearm while she clutched the handset.

"Yes. This is Sarah Hall," she said softly. Her face brightened, just for a moment, and she began to relax. Then she frowned.

"Oh ... I see...I see..." Her arm tensed as she gripped the phone. I pictured dark cells like tadpoles with sharp teeth swimming through her veins just below the surface.

"And there's no doubt, Doctor?... yes... thank you."

After she hung up, she turned to face me and just sort of held on, limp and slight in my arms. I wanted to say something, but I couldn't focus, couldn't talk. I looked over her shoulder at the fridge and the pink heart magnet that Emily had picked out for Sarah on Mother's Day. It was holding up one of Emily's famous letters. I looked over at Emily, who seemed absorbed in her drawing. She didn't talk much. She communicated mostly by writing letters. This one was addressed to the cat:

DEAR MUFFIN.

PLEES DON'T PEE IN MOM'S SHOE CLOSSET ANY

MORE.

WHEN THE TOWES GET SOGGIE YOU SEE THE

SLIPPERS ARE RUWINED.

I LL HELP YOU THROUGH THE CAT DOOR ANY

TIME YOU LIKE.

JUST MEOW FIRST, PLEES,

THANK YOU.

EMILY HALL

P.S. ALL THE SAME YOU ARE A VERRY GOOD CAT.

Each time I tried to say something to Sarah, I stopped myself, thinking of the man who says *I know how you feel* to his wife while she is in labor. After a while of just holding her, I led her upstairs to our bedroom, out of earshot of Emily. I told Sarah I would be right beside her, no matter what. I was scared. I pretended not to be. I thought I had carried it off quite well, but Sarah could tell.

I put Emily to bed that night.

"Daddy, why can't mommy read me a story tonight? I want a story."

"I'll read to you, Angelface," I said. "Which one do you want?"

"I want mommy to read."

"Mommy's tired tonight. Daddy will read to you". Emily looked up at me with her blue eyes that could look through me and that could hold my gaze unblinking far longer than I could hold hers. She was studying me. I thought she might pout or climb out of her little sleigh bed and run into our bedroom where Sarah was still sobbing quietly, but instead she smiled, and her smile grew wider and wider until all I could see were her teeth and her gums. For just that moment, the terror in my head abated, and I felt as though Emily had stroked my face.

"It'll be okay Daddy," she said finally. Something in the far-off way she said this made me wonder if she was still talking about who would read her the book, but I had a sense that it wasn't. Then her tone changed back again.

"You read then Daddy. Pooh might sound funny with you reading." In a while, her face relaxed into sleep as she sank into the pillow. I remembered the first time Sarah had called her Angelface. A few weeks old, she had been sleeping in her crib. "Look at her, Sam," Sarah had said. "What can she be smiling at?" I had leant over the crib beside Sarah. Emily's eyes were tight shut, and there was a broad grin on her tiny face.

"Some tired old joke," I had suggested.

"She must remember it from the time before she was born, then." Sarah had said, leaning further over the crib.

"Who told her it, do you think? Angels?" I had asked, watching as Emily's smile widened still further.

"Angels." Sarah had said. "Do you think she is an angel?" Then she had bent down to kiss Emily on the forehead. "Sleep tight, Angelface."

The next five months after the phone call were a blur of chemotherapy and doctors and support groups. The main focus, Sarah and I decided, must be to protect Emily from all this. Oh, we knew what the books said: truth is best, even hard truth. We agreed with this, but not yet. Not until later. There would be time later. When Sarah had to give up her ballet classes, she just told Emily that she was tired and needed a break. Emily seemed to accept it, although she stopped wearing her pink ballet slippers. Emily seemed oblivious; especially cheerful, even. I realized she hadn't had a tantrum or a pouting spell since the night of the call. We put this down to a new phase in her development.

A couple of weeks into June, Sarah began to get her appetite back. She told me she was feeling less tired, and the color in her cheeks began to reappear. She was hopeful, and so was I. In front of her. Underneath, I didn't dare to be. I had read all about false remissions. We had been going for long walks together in the sunshine, which could easily explain all these signs. On the next visit to the doctor, his usually somber manner changed as he reviewed the bloodwork. I thought I even detected surprise in his voice. Through August and into early fall, the doctor's surprise yielded to cautious hope, then optimism and then, unbelievably, to certainty. It was over. Definitely, absolutely over.

On one of the last visits to the doctor's office, Sarah and I were sitting side by side in the chairs that had borne us through so much over the past few months. From across his desk, the doctor pulled open a drawer, took out a folded letter, and handed it to Sarah. He smiled.

"This came in January."

I watched Sarah's face as she unfolded it and started to read. When she had finished, she covered her eyes with her hand and passed it to me without looking up.

DEAR DOCTOR JONSON,

I HOPE IT IS ALRITE THAT I AM SENDI NG YOU

THIS LETTER. MY MOM IS VERY

SPESHAL TO ME OR I WOOD NOT RITE THIS

LETTER TO YOU.

I NO YOU CAN MAKE MOM BETTER IF YOU TRY

YOUR VERRY VERRY

HARDEST.

PLEES MAKE HER BETTER.

YOURS TRULY.

EMILY HALL

P.S. PLEES DON'T TELL MOM OR DAD THAT I NO

THAT MOM IS SICK AS THEY ARE VERRY KIND

AND DO NOT WANT ME TO BE SAD.

Chapter 15

Body of Work

The writer shapes the contours of the body of her work.

She lays out one small fragment on each page.

The reader feels the writer's gentle pen on every page.

The writer feels the reader read her words.

The reader's eyes study the writer's past,

and feel her stifled life that no one knew.

He burrows for her tale, and peels away the layers

between the calloused covers of her book.

Whole chapters startle, imperfections jut and jar,

and bring out all the pain of his own aches.

Her story takes him back

to all the scenes of verbal beatings,

the fists of accusations, for things he never did.

The reader and the writer hold each other tightly,

then share their stifled horrors

that are not any secrets anymore.

And, when they read her words aloud together,

side-by-side,

they feel the demons writhe under the covers of their bed.

At last, those vengeful ghosts steal out,

and with their bag of tricks, all disappear.

PART THREE

SHATTERED

THE PAIN WE SHARE

Chapter 16

Stars and Stripes

9/11

On Rockefeller Center

in the Tuesday morning breeze

a flag that broadcasts freedom

flies proudly and at ease.

As New York City wakens

and rubs its sleepy eyes,

a darkness and a shaking

and a wailing fill the skies.

And, moving like a rocket,

a rat runs in the road

and, racing past the reeling flag

runs headlong for uptown.

By dusk the flag is weeping

at the sky and at the ground

three thousand new stars shining,

and two less stripes downtown.

Chapter 17

The Lucky Tie

September 11, 2001

In a house on a street in New Jersey,

in the kitchen, a dad starts his day,

and he brews up a big pot of coffee,

and moves the cat out of his way.

On the front porch, he stoops for the paper;

this Tuesday the headlines are dull.

He sets it aside to read later

and heads for the shower down the hall.

At the girls' open door, the dad pauses.

The sound of their breathing is deep;

in the dark room, the rock stars and horses

watch over their beds as they sleep.

In the bathroom the dad begins shaving,

decides that he likes his own smile,

and that, if he's good about flossing,

he'll hold off the crowns for a while.

In the bedroom, he touches his wife's sleeping head;

an expression of peace on her face.

Her hand is stretched out to his side of the bed,

as though she is saving his place.

In silence, he puts on his suit for downtown

and the tie the girls gave him for luck –

the one with the horseshoes and ponies and clowns

and the elephant driving a truck.

Then he kisses his sleeping children

and whispers goodbye to his wife

and takes the first train to Manhattan

on this, the last day of his life.

Chapter 18

Bottom Land

I T'S FALL, 1994. I am in my conference room, trying to forget that there is a message from my mother in my slot at the reception desk. She only calls if she has bad news. She saves the good news for her letters. I am sort of glad that it is one o'clock in the morning in London, so I can't call her back until tomorrow.

The last light of the San Francisco day fades as I set the trowel down on the sill. I stand back and study the half-planted row of English yews in the window box outside the conference room window. As planned, the dark, spiky leaves block my view of the Stock Exchange's ugly roof through the window. I feel sorry for the yews. They are a long way from their native countryside. I wonder how they feel about their disappointing new home. They must know that they will not live long in their windswept, grimy graves.

I always do my paperwork and odd jobs at the office on Saturdays. This weekend I am lingering over the tasks. I don't have to get home at any special time. Beth is in Connecticut again, visiting her sick father, and the kids are off at camp. Saturdays are the only days that are just about bearable for me downtown, with the empty streets swept clean by the morning fog, the sidewalks free of the weekday faces, wearing their hunted scowls like masks in some dark pantomime. The car horns and fumes have suspended themselves, and the faint smell of the sea reminds me of the Suffolk coast. It's the weekdays that I dread downtown. The laughs with no laughter; e-mail and voicemail that I can never quite empty; the flatness of success.

Lately, downtown reminds me of dad. Bowler hat and sensible tie. A slave to alcohol under the hopeless yoke of a Civil Service job in London. Mornings like a coal miner in the Underground commute, even down to the tunnels. Nights too tired to smile. It eventually killed him.

Beth has been ready for years to have me quit. She was raised on a farm in Oregon. We did all the research long ago. Organic farming. I have encouraged it. She has studied for it at U.C. Davis, and volunteers at Green Gulch farm north of San Francisco. But the time to make the break never comes. Now we almost never talk about it. I sense her disappointment, and it embarrasses me. I have no excuse for what I do now with my life. What if I look back in twenty, thirty years, only for this to be all there has been? I go out to the front desk again and pick up the receptionist's handwritten message.

Your mom called.

She is *mother* and, sometimes, *mum*, but never *mom*. She hates to be called *mom*, especially by me. Because it means that I really did move to

America fifteen years ago, and I'm not just on an *extended holiday*, as she told her friends for the first ten years at least. Handwritten messages are rare since voicemail was installed, but mother has never trusted voicemail, which she calls *answer phones*. She can't accept the one-sidedness of it all.

"It's so *rude*, Adrian dear. If I call someone, I expect to speak to a person, not a machine. Either they are in, or they are out. Yes? So, if they are out, then I can call them later when they are in. If they are in, they should jolly well pick up the telephone when it rings, unless they are invalids."

This is, of course, all a front. Mother is hard of hearing and confused by technology. When she first used to call my voicemail, she would try to engage it in conversations that I would save and replay for weeks afterwards.

"Adrian, darling, it's you. I'm so glad I caught you... Now, how are Elizabeth and the children? Adrian? Adrian?..."

She deliberately calls Beth *Elizabeth*. "*Beth's* so *American*," she says. And she dislikes the fact that Queen Elizabeth could one day possibly be called *Beth*.

This voicemail confusion sort of thing happened several times, but eventually she stopped trying. I miss these interludes, but not the cajoling about my brother.

"Jeremy's business is doing so well here. The Kew house is so convenient for the City. Why can't you give up this *American* thing, Adrian? You would fit back in as if you had never left, dear."

I settle in a chair with my feet up on the windowsill, lean back, and breathe in the rich scent of the potting soil.

The smell takes me back to the summers in the garden in Suffolk with my big brother. Jeremy and I had both understood clearly then that life was meant to be lived outdoors. The countryside had been no more than a boyhood interlude for the two of us, but it has stayed with me forever. A cheap cottage on the featureless Suffolk coast, as flat as a Dutch landscape; the hardest place in the world to get to from London.

Sitting by the open fire one winter's evening, in the little front room of the cottage, Jeremy had been poring over an atlas.

"You know, Ade, England looks just like a running man with a big backside."

I squinted over. He had a point.

"Guess where we are?" He pointed to our village, right at the place where the buttocks protruded the most.

"Bottom Land," he grinned. The name stuck.

It was to become our haven. Despite the drive from London before Motorways, a hundred miles that took five hours in the sweltering heat. Despite the smell of vegetables in the back of the Zephyr station wagon; the pugdog's slobber and the stench of his breath; the smoke from dad's unfiltered Navy Cut cigarettes. Despite Jeremy and me fighting for control of the windows, of the front seat, of the furthest spot from the dog's breath.

"Boys, will you *stop* fighting, and look at the view!" mum would say. Dad was mostly silent.

The best was the relief of getting there. Finally. Jumping out of the car at Bottom Land and being overtaken by the fresh-made air in the still summer night. A giant sky speckled with the stars you never saw in London because of the orange glow that clogged the air. Jeremy would wake me up the next morning and drag me out of bed to see what had grown out of our spring seeds. Multicolored hollyhocks and orange nasturtiums. Carrots and beets. The lettuces that we would pick, with earth trodden into their limp leaves. Mum and dad would leave them on the sides of their plates, but they tasted so good to Jeremy and me.

Friday nights, mother would take me and Jeremy to meet dad from the London steam train. He would step onto the platform followed by a swirl of smoke and dust. He looked so pale and out of place in his bowler hat, carrying a gladstone bag with his office work in it.

Mother called us her *little earthworms* because we would dig and dig in the garden just for the sake of it. For the feel of the cold, damp earth on our hands. One day Jeremy was standing over me on the edge of a hole we had been digging. I was leaning on a spade looking up at his dirty face, framed against the sky. He had a handful of earth in his open palm.

"Ade, have you ever thought? I bet no one ever dug this earth before." He picked out a small stone.

"No one put this here, not mum or dad or teachers. It's just ... here." It made me feel special. Jeremy thought of things that no one else would, and he wanted to share them with me. I followed Jeremy everywhere.

Bentwaters was the American Air Force base a few miles from the cottage. Jeremy had been listening to the planes overhead all summer and decided to find out where they were landing. He disappeared one morning on his bicycle. When he came back in the late afternoon, he was excited.

"Ade, you've got to come with me tomorrow. The pilots are ace. You never saw anything go like those Starfires." His green eyes danced, and his face shone. I felt thrilled. It was always that way. He lifted me up to his level whatever we did together.

"Don't say anything to mum and dad," he added.

The next day, we cycled off to the base. We hid our bikes in the hedge at the roadside. Jeremy wiggled on his belly under the perimeter fence and motioned for me to follow.

"We can't, it's dangerous."

"Chick-chick-chicken," Jeremy shouted back. "They're closing the base next year. This'll be our last chance." He had crawled away before I could answer. I followed him because I had no choice. I was scared. We waited on our bellies for what seemed like forever. I was terrified that someone would see us and put us in prison. After a while, I could hear a faint rumble in the distance.

"Ade. Do you hear that? They're coming." The sound turned into a growl and then grew to a roar. A triangle of eight red fighters flashed across the pale blue of the Suffolk sky. They were coming in from the sea at absurd speeds with parachutes billowing behind, landing now at close intervals, so close that I thought I could see the concentration on the pilots' faces. The scream of the jets and the smell of the burnt tires biting into the runway made me feel like running. I looked over at Jeremy beside me in the grass a few yards away, with his freckled, sunny face watching the last of the planes. He turned toward me, gave me a thumbs up and grinned. The slipstream from the jet tousled his hair. He scrambled over, hugged me like a wrestler, and threw me onto the grass at the end of the runway. Suddenly I felt safe. After that, we went back every chance we could get. The next summer, we went back one last time. The base had closed, and the runway had sprouted weeds.

The airmen and their families lived in Bottom Land. This was my first exposure to Americans, and I was entranced. Their cars, tail fins as large as whale flukes, poked out of the driveways of the tiny houses and protruded a few feet into the street, so that dad had to swerve the Zephyr to the center of the road to navigate around them. One day, Jeremy sneaked a sun yellowed Spiderman comic book off the back seat of a parked Cadillac and showed it off to me in the field behind the cottage. I was fascinated by the ads for Tootie Roll Pops and magic rings. The English comics, Beano, Eagle, Beezer, Dandy, had too few pictures, and the characters were the kind of people your parents knew, and you might meet on the street anyway. At the other end of the scale, they were ludicrously unbelievable superheroes or World War II soldiers. There was Sergeant Sam, who called the Japanese soldiers *little yellow perishers*, Desperate Dan, who was a musclebound version of the Hulk and ate *cow pie*. Billy Whizz, Dan Dare, who battled the Mekon, a ruthless alien who had six-foot antennae and two heads, one green and the other blue. There was one character I liked, Denis the Menace, because he was just like Jeremy, with a mop of black hair and a nose for finding trouble. The American comics allowed you to believe there was a larger, more colorful world out there. That men could fly in disguise. Superman and Spiderman and Batman. I think it was soon after that I decided that I would live in America one day. I opened my textbook during a fifth form geography lesson, and there was a picture of wheat fields in Wisconsin. I pictured myself driving a red Cadillac as big as a whale with two huge tail flukes through the giant golden landscape.

Jeremy chose New Zealand about the same time. "Sheep farming, Ade. Sixty million sheep, bro, and only two million people. Fresh lamb every day, and no thieving brothers to beat me to the second helping." I tried to laugh when he said that, but I remember being frightened. I had never thought about being separated from him before. Later, when he wasn't looking, I sneaked a look at the atlas, to see how far New Zealand was from America. It was far. After dinner, looking across the table at him, I choked up and had to excuse myself.

Somehow, Jeremy never made it to New Zealand. After university, on impulse, he married Jenny. She was already pregnant. Also on impulse, he took the first job offer he got at the graduate career fair as a trader at an oil company in the City.

"Just temporary, Ade. Anyway, it is a sort of farming. Oil, mutton, wool, same difference. Just remember now bro, *stay alive, no nine to five.*" That was our saying in those days.

The year I left for San Francisco, Jenny got pregnant again, and Jeremy bought a house in Kew, just outside London.

"Just an investment, Ade, house market's booming. I'll flog it next year, take the cash and buy that farm." He never even came close.

I stretch my arms and break my daydream. The yews are silhouetted against a darkening sky. I find it hard to believe it has been 20 years since Jeremy bought that house. Hard to believe he still trades oil in the City of London. These days when I go back, he doesn't like to talk about the old dream. About New Zealand or farming or escape. He teases me about my own fading plans.

"Well, if it isn't my hayseed bro Ade from 'Frisco. You growing taters downtown? Mushrooms on the rug? Rice in the bathtub?" I fancy there is something new in his tone now, a bitterness under the laugh. Maybe I don't know Jeremy too well anymore. Sometimes I just about get to thinking he's okay with his life. Then I think back to Suffolk, of how trapped I feel myself downtown, even in America, and I think *no, he's not okay with it.*

I look around the conference room at the photographs and the plaques. Buildings I have sold. Deals I have made, faster than anyone could imagine. For more money than I can fathom. They still call me the British Hurricane. Arranged in neat rows are the thirty leather-backed chairs where I sit through meetings with my brokers and clients. Endless meetings. The *Adrian Pryor* Company logo that Beth had first sketched at our kitchen table fifteen years ago is everywhere. So is the company declaration:

> We have a *Pryor* Commitment.
>
> our clients first, not us.
>
> -Adrian M. Pryor

It seems so trite and foolish now.

I decide to finish the window boxes, kill some time with paperwork, and grab something to eat downtown. I can go back to the office and call mum around 11 P.M. She will be up by then, 7 A.M. Greenwich Meantime, getting ready for church. *Meantime*, as if England is where people pass the time until their real lives begin somewhere else.

I eat a late dinner in North Beach and drive back to the dark office building around 10:45. The streets are deserted as I unlock the great art deco door and step into the chapel-like lobby. On my way up in the elevator, I think again about the call I must make. Maybe it is just a problem with the central heating again, the timer on the thermostat most likely. Winter is approaching and mum is alone in the drafty house by the

Thames. I shiver, but I can't decide whether it's the thought of an English winter, or because I'm dreading the call.

I go into the conference room, pick up the phone, and dial. She answers almost at once, as if she has been waiting by the phone. It isn't the thermostat.

"Darling, I have to tell you something." She sounds dreadful.

I shiver again. "What is it, mum?"

"I'm so sorry." Her voice wavers, "So dreadfully sorry." I can hear her sobbing. "It's Jeremy, dear."

I start to shake. Outside, a breeze buffets the yews. "You see, I think he must have been terribly unhappy."

Half listening as she continues, I think of the red jets over Bentwaters, banking high and wide against a blue Suffolk sky, and heading out to sea.

Chapter 19

I Hate December

I hate the winter, God I hate the cold.

God damn December

and God damn this rain.

Why did I ever like it, was it you?

the hands-in-hands, the sweater that you wore,

the way you laughed at me when I fell down

and lay before you on the sodden ground.

Well, now that season's sneered and slunk away,

and left me with its echo mocking me.

It's left me with its windswept grimy streets,

its wetness and its hard, unsmiling grey.

It's made me stay behind to smell the rain.

And now you haunt this empty broken town.

Chapter 20

Kensington Gardens

So blue, so cold and blue,

this London sky stings through the leaf-shed park,

and I, just passing through, who yearn to be so warm,

just cold and dark remain.

No, I'm not glad to wander in this winter hush alone.

So white, so crisp and white,

the seagulls on the pond spread wings and fly,

as though they know a height

where memories of you have room to die.

Well, I will never fly with them to drift and climb

and close my mind

to summer's vanished leaves.

Chapter 21

Gray

IT WAS IN 1954 that Kevin first felt ashamed of his dad. The teacher was going around the eighteenth-century classroom in the grammerschool for boys in London. She was asking the seven-year-olds what their fathers did for a living. All Kevin knew was what his mother had told him.

"Your father works for the government, dear. He's a Civil Servant. His job is really *quite* important."

The boys were sitting in rows of upright wooden desks, carved with the initials of six generations. Kevin was sitting next to Johnnie Parker, the son of the local Jaguar dealer.

"And Kevin, what does *your* father do?"

"He's a civil servant." Kevin said. He paused for effect. "With *special* duties." A squeaking voice broke in.

"No he ain't." It was Johnnie Parker. "That's a fib. He's a janitor down at the Town Hall. My old man says so."

A silence followed. Kevin waited for the teacher to contradict Johnnie, but she just smiled and quickly moved on. Kevin flushed, and his eyes watered.

After class, the November sky glowered down on the playground, still wet underfoot with mushy leaves. A voice came from behind him.

"What's your dad do, Kevin? Him with the limp."

'Big fat Johnnie Parker, Johnnie PORKER', Kevin said to himself.

Parker and his cronies crowded around.

"I'm talking to *you,* dodo brain. What's *he do,* Kevin?" Kevin looked at the ground, where a mud puddle reflected a wavering image of his school cap and the heavy sky behind him.

"Say it, Kevin," Parker leered. *"Janitor.* Say it. Pretty good around toilets. I hear he's handy around *shit. "*

Kevin didn't answer. Parker shoved him with the flat of his hand and he fell to his knees in the water. He didn't cry, not then. He got up quickly and walked to the perimeter wall, where the wind swirling down gave his eyes an excuse for tears. *Airline pilot. Racing Car Driver.*

He walked home to the little brick terraced council house. He cleaned himself up. Later, he ate toast and Marmite and Heinz baked beans in the kitchen with his mother.

'What's dad really do, mum? He's not a *janitor or* anything, is he?"

Slowly, his mother laid down her knife and fork and stopped chewing. She turned her thin, nervous face towards him and looked at him carefully. Finally, she said,

"*Custodian,* dear, is the word I prefer. I married your father because he is a fine man. He loves you very much, you know dear."

Janitor, janitor, janitor.

From then on, Kevin decided he would lie about his father.

Complicated fibs. He's *incognito. He* can't *reveal what he does. Not even to me and mum. Affairs of state depend on it. Matters of national importance.* He got these phrases from accounts of the Russian spy trials in the British papers. Kim Philby; Donald Maclean.

He buried himself in schoolwork, especially English, and his teachers began to praise him. One winter night, not long after the playground incident, Kevin was lying scrunched up tight in bed, hugging his knees. Outside, a freezing wind buffeted the windowpane. The reflection of the plane trees blowing in the back yard threw a pattern of quaking shadows on the ceiling. Off in the distance, London's traffic splashed busily. He heard the bedroom door squeak open and sensed his father standing over him. *Please let him think I'm asleep.* Kevin felt his breath, thick and sour; the smell that had become as much a part of his dad as his voice or his face.

Kevin lay still and breathed deeply. He felt his father's finger stroke his cheek as he whispered, "Night, night, genius. Making your daddy proud, you are." The words came with a stutter, the way he always spoke, but when he smelled this way, they also came with a slur. As he left the room, he must have stumbled, because the chair by the bed scraped across the floor. Other nights, his dad came in and spoke to him in rhyming verse in the darkness. "If you learn your lessons well, you will ring the victory bell. If you learn your lessons right, you will fly high as a kite."

His father did a lot of reading when he wasn't asleep or at work. The bookshelf in the living room bulged with classics; Dickens, Austen, Bronte, Forster. And poetry. Volumes of poetry. Kevin once pulled out a thick novel and found hidden behind it a small edition called *Poems of the Great War*. His father's name was on the *Ex Libris* sticker in the flyleaf. Dog-eared, thumbed and grimy, Thomas Gray and Wilfred Owen and Rupert Brooke had been read, read, and reread, until the stitching had come undone. John Gillespie Maggee, who had died flying a Spitfire in the Battle of Britain. He had just turned nineteen.

> *Oh! I have slipped the surly bonds of Earth*
> *and danced the skies on laughter-silvered wings.*

And Rupert Brooke who was killed in the trenches in World War I.

> *If I should die, think only this of me;*
> *that there's some corner of a foreign field*
> *that is forever England.*

Opposite the house was a bombsite where a church had once been. His mother said a V-2 rocket had landed there one Christmas morning near the end of the war, halfway through the sermon. Weeds choked the ankles of the soaring stone arches, which now supported only sky. The year Kevin turned thirteen, they had rebuilt the church with plain, economical brickwork. When it opened, Kevin's dad became a verger on Sundays, as he had been in the old building before it was bombed. Since he never mentioned God, and since Kevin never saw him praying, he decided he only did it to please his mother.

On the way into church one Sunday, an old lady wearing a mangy mink and reeking of mothballs looked at Kevin through her veil and said, "It's so nice to see your father back at church again. Used to read the lessons you know, dear. Such a *fine* reading voice he used to have before...in the old days."

His father walked slowly down the nave of the church with the collection plate, his game leg dragging. Kevin pretended to be praying and peeked out between his fingers to see if people were staring at his dad. The old ladies with the wavering voices were the worst; they had pity in their stares. His dad just smiled at them and seemed not to notice. Kevin wanted him, just once, to stare back. The optimism in the hymns seemed all to do with the great joys in store after death, before which time there was no hope. Beside him, his mother sang her way through every word. "Miserable sinners...we have left undone those things which we ought to have done...done those things which we ought not to have done...we are not fit so much as to gather up the crumbs under thy table."

His mother sang a lot around the house, too. Hymns mostly, but there was one opera she loved, and often in the evenings she sang it: *"Oh for the wings for the wings for the wings of a dove...*with dad snoring in his armchair...to *carry me...far away, far away."* Over the years the chair cover where his dad's head rested had become soiled with the grime of the Town Hall.

The peaceful times back then were the few nights when his father came in early and stayed awake, sitting with his mother in the living room long after Kevin had gone to bed, their muffled talk a low, even murmur. Their voices rising and falling through his bedroom door reminded him of the dark surf breaking on the shores of the North Sea where they would sometimes go camping for summer holidays.

One night from the living room his mother's voice shrilled out, "Always making excuses for you...drink is the *devil's* sustenance...why can't you bury the past like those it belongs to?" His dad's reply was too faint to hear. Maybe he didn't reply.

Dad often asked Kevin about school; it was the only thing he ever really questioned him about. Kevin was doing better and better. He wrote stories with ever more complex plots, and these tales helped him perfect his lies about his dad. *Working for Special Branch at Government House. Deep underground.* Somehow, this fit with his father's pale skin and colorless suits.

After prep school, Kevin was sent to a government grammar school. Then he won a scholarship to an expensive private school in London, all fees paid. His father hugged him so hard he couldn't breathe. Saint Paul's School lay in the shadow of the great cathedral. One Thursday night during the Blitz, the Luftwaffe had targeted the cathedral. A bomb fell through the ancient dome but didn't detonate. It just lay there like an offering on the stone floor of the great nave. The square mile around the cathedral was razed bare in the barrage of that night.

His father couldn't drive, so Kevin's mother would pick him up after school in her battered Morris Minor. School let out at 3:00. Kevin told her 3:30 so the other boys wouldn't see the car drive up. He had a sweet tooth, but he never had the money for chocolate at the school shop. Other boys bailed him out all the time. Kevin developed a sense of humor. He felt like a jester earning his food; a buffoon for his friends, but never an equal. Still, he earned his keep.

Kevin learned about the war in history class. How Churchill and Roosevelt, and Field Marshal Montgomery, who had gone to his school, *crushed the Hun and the Nip with valor and never counted the cost,* and he wondered what his dad did in it. He was afraid to ask him. Afraid because he couldn't picture him as being brave at all. More of a man who had an excuse; high blood pressure or something. At least by not asking he could pretend. When he finally did bring it up, the year before he finished school, he surprised himself by just coming out and asking his mother in the kitchen. She was making dinner. She turned the black knob on the enamel stove down to *simmer.*

"The war, darling, is not discussed in this house."

"What do you mean not *discussed?*"

"Exactly that. The war was a bad thing. It hurt a lot of good people. Inside and out."

"But dad was in the war, wasn't he? Isn't that how he hurt his leg? How he got the stutter?"

"Kevin. That's enough!"

"Mum, please. Just say-was he in it?"

"Yes! Yes, yes, yes, yes! Enough!!"

"But why can't we talk about it? I'm his son. I've a right to know."

"You have no rights; no rights unless I say so. Honor thy father and mother. That includes obey."

"Suit yourself! I'll ask dad then."

Kevin stomped towards the door. He had never seen his mother lose control before. Now he heard a tone in her voice beyond all limits; like an animal hit by a car.

So Kevin left it alone.

He discovered girls and motorcycles about this time. And booze. The smell of whisky on the breath of his drinking buddies. The familiarity of the smell dawned on him, more like a slowly clearing fog than a sudden flash.

Alcoholic had never been said, but now he felt the word envelop the house like an ether. It had seeped into everything like sewage in a flood. During this time, his parents irritated him. His father was a shadow man. The gray man. Evenings he came in late smelling of Cutty Sark and slept in his chair in the living room until eleven or midnight and then went to bed. Most nights his place was empty at the dinner table, with him asleep in the living room. When he stirred, he would say, "Time for bed," and then go back to sleep.

"Oh David," Kevin heard his mother say one night through the living room door. "I'd be less lonely with you not here at all." His father didn't answer her. Through the crack in the door, Kevin saw him fussing with his stained woolen tie, loosening it and tightening it, and then fall back to sleep.

At eighteen, Kevin won a scholarship to Oxford. When the letter arrived one Saturday morning in spring with the Oxford seal on it, his father brought it to him with the London Times. Kevin knew he was waiting for him to open the letter so he deliberately put it down and started in on the newspaper. When his father had gone back to the living room, he tore open the envelope, read the letter and kissed it. Presently there was a knock at the door and his father came back in. The stuttering was more pronounced than normal, the way it would get when he wanted to say something important.

"Kevin. Son, I know you aren't very proud of your old man. I know that. Me neither, truth told."

Kevin thought his father was going to leave again because he turned away from him. But he continued, "If that letter says what I think it does, God, Kevin. Son, if it makes a difference...you're my pride." He shuffled up to Kevin and hugged him hard, pressing an envelope into his hand. Kevin pulled out a check for £200. On the reference line it said, in his father's scrambled handwriting: For purchase of one Triumph motorcycle. Kevin looked up.

"Dad, this is too much. Does mum know? You don't have the money to spare. At least make it a loan, not a gift."

"Keep it, son. It's for you. Not doing any good stuck in a bank."

Kevin's mother was listening from the kitchen, where she was making hot cross buns for Lent. She watched every penny his father spent. Without her, they would not even have enough to eat. She said, "I expect Kevin really wants to pay it back, David. It's quite generous, even as a loan." His dad fell silent. Kevin folded the check and left the room.

The Triumph suited the Oxfordshire lanes. The angry sound it made and the smell of hot oil on the foot pegs mirrored Kevin's mood. He got a summer job helping set up exhibits at the Ashmolean Museum and earned back the £200 by the last week of the summer. He mailed his father a check from Oxford at the start of the autumn term.

At Christmas, Kevin came back and was struck by the somberness of the house. His room was just as he had left it in August, one curtain drawn co keep the morning sun off the pillow. But now, in mid-winter, the sun never made it over the plane trees at the back of the house. A frost lingered on the lawn and the windows stayed fogged up all day. His father had not been to work for six weeks. He rarely left his chair now. In February, after Kevin had been back in Oxford for a few weeks, his mother called, quite calm. He even detected a hint of relief in her tone as she said, "Your father died in his sleep last night." Kevin got home to find her in the kitchen. She seemed steadfast during the funeral and the week afterwards, although Kevin fancied her gray eyes were looking through him rather than at him.

Three years passed, and his mother crumbled. When Kevin visited during the last of those days, she seemed so much smaller than before. In the end, she would just sit in her chair opposite the living room window looking out at London's grayness, and mouth words for days at a time. They could have been Hail Mary's or prayers. Kevin covered up her legs with a blanket. Soon he was signing the papers to admit her into a nursing home. The house seemed like a dead body whose spirit had vacated. It was time to sell it. Cleaning out his father's writing desk, Kevin opened a drawer. There he found a small royal blue leather case, stamped with the Royal Airforce R.A.F. insignia, with his father's initials on it. Inside was a medal, the Victoria Cross, the V.C. the highest honor in the land, awarded for valor in the presence of the enemy.

By the time Kevin had finished with the drawer, his father was a different man: a discharge for medical reasons, with honors; a photograph of him in a flying suit on a grass airfield somewhere in England with one hand on the wing of a Spitfire. A bundle of letters to mother from a hospital in Scotland, written in his father's firm, strong handwriting, in HB pencil with almost no corrections. A collection of poems, dogeared until 1943 and never resumed. A photograph of his father astride a Brough Superior motorcycle outside St. John's College, Oxford. If his mother had had a drawer, Kevin wondered whether it would have contained questions or answers. After he closed the door to the house for the last time, he pulled from his pocket his father's wallet. Inside it, uncashed, wrinkled, and smudged, was the check Kevin had written to him for £200.

Chapter 22

Her Spare Hand

I WAS HAPPY WITH Sarah in a way that might have lasted a lifetime. Our children were sunny and secure. Our lovemaking was sublime, infused with an honesty borne of trust.

On Tuesday, I drove home early from downtown San Francisco, just wanting to be with them that shining September afternoon. The sun was playing strobe through the railings on the Golden Gate Bridge.

Suddenly, in front of me, I recognized Sarah's VW Bug, with the *Carpe Diem* sticker in the window.

I drew level, to catch her attention and make her smile with the joy of seeing me.

That was when I noticed her passenger, and her spare hand, as it explored his curly black hair.

PART FOUR

SORROW IN SUNLIGHT

LIFE'S LAMENTS

Chapter 23

Death of an Oarsman

The water stretched out its dark surface

like a sheet of black cloth on the Bay,

and the wind was dawn's sleeping accomplice,

bringing stillness to usher the day.

A spell that we didn't want broken

came down like a mist from the hills.

In the boat not a sentence was spoken

and even the coxswain was still.

In the silence, we felt our friend's presence

as we covered a magical mile,

and the moon was an upturned crescent

as it hung in the sky like a smile.

He was the rushing sound our bow made

and the balance that flowed through our feet,

and the even wake our hull left

as the current slipped under our seats.

By the light of the sun as it rose

from the lull of the boat's gentle glide

we knew, though the man might be gone,

still his spirit was sculling beside.

We know, though the man might be gone,

still his spirit is sculling beside.

Chapter 24

Fifty-Four Roadster

This Man at Forty

The party's over early, we drive home.

Tonight my wife makes me feel old

by looking young to me and being, frankly,

every bit my age.

Her card says *forty-life has just begun.*

I ask her what she means.

She tells me, "What it says,"

and gives my hand a squeeze.

We reach the house, it's dark. I let the motor run.

"We need some beer and milk," I say.

"Back soon."

She says "ok."

I'm tired of driving,

stomping on the gas,

the road's flown by so fast.

My skid marks tell the tale.

Twenty pulled over,

letting thirty pass,

as forty, tucked unseen behind,

slipstreamed, then made its move.

Big dreams transformed to maybes,

turned to maybe nots.

Now time elapsed surpasses time to come,

and spunk feels caution's foot apply the brakes.

I flee downtown,

seek shelter from the clock,

and park the Honda, stumble out,

and strain to hear the action just a block away.

The glow from clubland shimmers -

phosphorescence on a darkened sea.

Behind me, streetlamps mark a landing strip

along the double-decade stretch I've flown.

Red carpet through the door at Crazy Ed's.

Testosterone crows lustily and brags;

short skirts and sex talk carry to the street.

My shadow tugs my jacket from behind.

The wind picks up and blows me past, not in;

a singer sings; the song is *Walk On By*.

My longing dies.

Belonging slams the door.

Was it *that* long ago,

year nineteen-fifty-four?

Chapter 25

Gone

As she exhales her last and softest sigh,

the window high above his sleeping wife

blows from its mouth a breeze of evening sky,

then draws into its lungs the end of life.

Alone now with the truth of how death is,

he sits with her, his wife, his constant friend.

Still clasping tight her hand that still clasps his,

he kneels and cries for pain that cannot mend.

Her water glass, half-drunk, stands by her bed,

her dressing gown hangs limply from the door,

each object in the room now bows its head,

dusk's shadows spill inside and soil the floor.

The smell of memories and potpourri;

where does rage go when no-one is to blame?

Kind friends have said this is how death must be;

a blow so private that it has no name.

Now she is gone, he thinks, *I have a choice,*

to sit around and listen for her voice,

and miss her every moment without cease

or follow her to try to find some peace.

He leans and whispers softly in her ear

with words all thin and brittle from the tears,

best words that none but he will ever hear,

fine words from silver tongue in silver years.

"It's getting late, my love, it's time for bed

you go ahead; I shan't be far behind."

Chapter 26

Vancouver Heron

Tie and dye sky

late, late in the day,

the curtain of night dropping down.

There used to be trees in this magical place

but now only roads mark the spot

and the lights of the cars

throw out parallel bars

as the drivers roar back to their homes.

And no one is looking.

No one is looking

above them, all hurrying home.

The world that they own

is a world of their own

encased in their comfortable shells.

The heron flies by, as there's nowhere to rest,

and nowhere to nest for the night.

It's time to fly by

and the heron flies by

as he does

as he does

every night.

Yes, time has flown by

for the heron and I

and now we are both out of date.

Chapter 27

Undercover

I wear a suit and tie

over my feathered wings,

afraid they'll find me out

because that is just

what I do.

In this uniform, I blend in

with all these smiling warriors,

full of boast.

I am a songbird

without a song because that is just

the way it is.

Bear hugs, handshakes, sports talk,

always one more drink because

that is just

what you have to do.

I am the boxer in the ring

crowd-pleasing and throwing punches,

because that is just

what this boxer does.

Now I throw fights

with no thought of winning,

fights I do not care about

against opponents who do,

because that is just

what they do.

I sit in meetings watching

women afraid to speak

to men who do not listen,

because that is just

what some men do.

My silenced power,

held captive by my wages,

dreams of a day these wings will beat,

and fly me out of here.

Because that is just

what I have to do.

Chapter 28
Stifled

So many letters written and unsent, so many words conceived, but never born, and still the need to write and speak remains, to stoke the fire of such an inner rage.

How can a shout so loud, a heat that burns white hot, be muted, stifled under such a cloth of pain, that even in the depths of lonely night no whisper breaks this lying veil of calm?

It remains to hope that somewhere
in the folds of time
is lodged the friendly gaoler's key
that will disturb this haunted peace
by freeing all the prisoners of this heart,
to call aloud the banner cries of love, and life.

Chapter 29
Sole Survivor

HOW DO YOU SAVE a lifeless marriage?

"Compromise," our therapist said, "meet in the middle."

"You mean stifle," I said.

I had first met Tracy eight years before, when I sat beside her at the annual faculty dinner at U.C. Berkeley. It was so random. I wasn't looking for someone. Nor was she. We were both in our early thirties, our careers flying. She had just published her first novel, and two of the top galleries in California had accepted my paintings. We were rising stars on the teaching staff at the University. Single, focused, and hungry.

But the decision was not ours to make. Fate had made the choice for us. I was pulled towards her in ways I could not understand. Her beauty, yes. Her smile and her wild dark hair. The Irish gypsy in her. I admired her mind. A writer, a reader, and a teacher. Soon it became obvious. We were in love. We moved in together after six months and got married soon after that. We bought our house a year later and christened it with a party to celebrate my new position as head of the Faculty for the Arts, and hers as Senior English Professor.

We laughed that our kids would have my ginger hair and one black eye like hers and one blue eye like mine. She was funny. Laugh-out-loud-snorting-milk-out-of-nostrils funny.

Eight years after that first meeting, the laughter had faded. Life seemed such a serious business. I remember thinking that Tracy and I had become two distinct species. Different animals entirely. Miss Safety and Mister Risk.

"Life is for consuming," I told her. "Why diet when your next bite might be your last?" Looking back on it, I realize it was an incredibly patronizing thing to say.

But I wanted it back. All of it. It had to be there somewhere, underneath the cobwebs and the dust and the tyranny of the urgent. I thought I just needed time to think. To work out how to recover what we once had. The steps to take.

One day we were standing on the balcony of our house in San Francisco's Sunset District. The fog had burned off and the midday sun had broken through. Standing there beside her, I considered reminding her about my dream of painting animals in the wild. The big cats. The leopards, cheetahs, and tigers. But that all felt selfish, unkind, dangerous. So I just came out and told her. I wanted to take a sabbatical from teaching to go round the world, to sort of '*clear my head.*'

Tracy looked startled and angry at the same time. "Is that a fact, David? Is that a goddamn fact?" She turned away and gripped the railing.

I remember shushing her for fear of reprisals from our neighbor, *Mister Radar Ears,* who was standing on his balcony in the house next door.

The more I shushed the more she raised her voice.

"So how much time are you thinking, mister wham–bam–thank–you–ma'am?"

It felt like I was cheating on her. This was hard, but I knew it would be hard. The words just came out now, as if someone else was speaking them. "Six months." I said.

"*Six months*!" she shouted over the rooftops at Mount Sutro. "Christ! And I suppose, Mister Born-To-Be-Wild, you're going to trot out the old '*if you love someone, set him free, and if it's meant to be, he will come back to you*'?"

"Shhh! Trace. It is not that long. Not logically, it's not. Not when you think in terms of the rest of our lives."

"What about in terms of me for a change! Mister fucking logical. What about thinking in terms of losing me? Suppose we think in terms of that."

I cringed at the *fucking* part. What if she wouldn't wait? The temptation to rewind and say I was not serious was overwhelming. But I knew I was too far in to get out. The damage was done. Even if I tried to mend things, to take it back, the shattered vase would always have a crack in it. "Trace. It is all right. Look..."

"No! It is just not all right. Not at all. You want to clear *your* head! Mine is clear as an ice cube. Clear that you are a selfish dick."

Now I look back on that Indian summer's day; the fog long burned off; the October sun baking the clay planter boxes of miniature roses that Tracy had nurtured during our years there. Our mountain bikes propped against the rail, saddles worn from the miles we had ridden together, exploring, and I can't imagine now how I had thought that a neighbor's eavesdropping could have been more important to me than holding on to what we had; more important than fighting for it at the top of my lungs. And I cannot imagine my arrogance in thinking she would sit still and wait to see if I came back to her. We didn't talk about it much after that. I guess she knew that if she pressed me, I would shut her out, so she shut me out instead, and I didn't try to break down the barrier. God, I must have been sure of myself. In bed, I would pull out my big cat books on India, Kenya, the Ngorongoro Crater in Tanzania, and Borneo–home of the Clouded Leopard, and pore over them. I would even ask her for advice. What was I *thinking*?

"David, I've *told* you. It's your trip. You've chosen not to include me, so don't expect me to get involved in the details. You're going, aren't you? Well, just go." She moved her things out and set up in her brother's house across the Golden Gate Bridge. She said it would make the eventual parting easier to bear if we separated in stages. She didn't ask me; she just went and did it. I was afraid. It seemed so final. I had lost control. She was the one making the decisions now. The tables had turned. She had the power, and I was the victim. I had to give up the stupid fantasy that she would keep our bed warm while I was gone. Trying to keep a physical connection between our lives, I did get her to hang one of my paintings at her brother's place; it was of a lone lion, one of the last, prowling the beach on the Skeleton Coast. I had called it a *self-portrait*.

"Your guardian," I said.

"Some guardian," she said. "In case you hadn't noticed, there's nobody for him to guard. He's alone."

I decided not to rent out the house. I couldn't stand the thought of a stranger in the place - it seemed like bad luck, as if some sort of spell might be broken.

A month later, when I was all packed and ready, she gazed at me over the backpacks and hiking gear scattered on the bed and said, "I've been doing some thinking, what with you going away, about what I want. Until now, I thought I pretty much knew." She went on to say that I was forty and she wasn't much younger. She said that looking for a soulmate is hard enough. She said we had found each other, which had saved us a lifelong search. Separating for six months was like discarding a diamond. She said more, but I didn't want to hear it, although there was one thing that stuck. "Traveling is lonely," she said, "Very lonely. You'll see." Then she added, almost under her breath, "But David, being the one left behind, that's worse. It leaves a gap that the person back home has to fill. With someone. Nature abhors a vacuum. I remember when my brother left home after mother died. It really changes you. You feel like the sole survivor of a family, a tribe, with no one to share the memories."

Well, traveling *was* lonely, and over the months away I felt Tracy slip from my reach down long-distance phone lines. In our conversations, I could measure the slippage by the lengthening pauses. The calls got shorter. I could not have asked for better views of some of the rarest of the big cats. I got close to Bengal Tigers, Ocelot, Jaguars. I painted in India, Africa, and Borneo. It was the realization of a dream, but it felt flat and anti-climactic. I remember thinking, '*what is wrong with me?*' I felt like a spoiled, ungrateful child.

Even then, I didn't feel urgency or panic. Not yet. I thought maybe it was just me-the jet lag and exhaustion that comes with crossing the globe and adjusting to heat and long-distance trekking; that our spiritual distance had a direct correlation with the physical miles between us, so that when I got back, with the separation over, our spirits would reconnect. I kept Tracy's picture tucked into my passport and studied it often. The kind smile. The dark, steady eyes. It was my antidote to fear.

Near the end of the long sabbatical, almost as an afterthought, I flew from Kuching in Borneo to Melbourne and took a small plane across the Tasman Sea to Hobart, the capital of Tasmania. On a map, Tasmania looks like a pebble cast off the southeastern shore of Australia, as though the thrower's fingers had slipped while executing a longer throw that would otherwise have gone right off the southern end of the world. This close to the South Pole, the sky is so bright you can't go without sunglasses. In many ways Tasmania is Australia's least important state, including population count and its fringe location. *Tazzie*, as Australians from the mainland sometimes call it, is often the butt of jokes; an outlandish, almost fictional place. Even its name might have been the invention of Tolkien or Swift. A fitting finale to the tale I would tell Tracy of my epic voyage, it suited the maverick image I cherished. But there is something sinister about the place. Its emptiness, with far more sheep than people, and its ghostly silver sky. By then it was late April, and the southern hemisphere was just turning the page from autumn to winter. One Sunday, the God-fearing shopkeepers had shuttered their stores, and the first storms were beating against the breakwaters. A lone church bell knelled. The church and a museum were the only two buildings open.

The museum in Hobart is a forlorn place. As I entered, the aluminum roof reflected the southern sky, harshly bright despite the rain that spanked the bare metal of the roof. The only other visitor was an old woman clutching a plastic handbag with a broken handle and mumbling. I picked up the cheaply typeset information sheet from the front desk. It told the story of the Tasmanian Aborigines and the Tasmanian Tigers and how they had both been hunted for sport and driven to extinction. It told how

Truganini, the last Tasmanian Aborigine, had lived on for five years as the solitary remnant of her race until her death in 1876 and how the last of tigers had disappeared by 1936, when the sole survivor, also female, had died in Hobart Zoo.

I moved through the museum. It was more like the storeroom above a back country taxidermist's shop. Decay and unconcern were everywhere. The label in front of the stuffed wallaby's case was torn and just said *Walla*. The horsehair filler was protruding from a rip in the head of the Tasmanian Devil, which was an unlikely mix of pig and raccoon. In a dark corner was a duck-billed platypus next to a spiny echidna. The plaque described the duo as the planet's only egg-laying mammals. Both of them looked like a collage of spare parts assembled by a thrifty god. I could picture the *great creator* muttering "waste-not want-not" as she worked. Both creatures had to have been a mistake made by an intoxicated carpenter after the lights had gone out in his workshop. The platypus's parents might have been a duck and a seal. It had the body of a seal with an enormous duck's bill jammed onto the end of its nose. The echidna was half hedgehog and half anteater, and its nose was clearly an afterthought, dead straight and as thin as a chopstick.

I found no Tasmanian Tiger, but just at the exit of the two-roomed building, in a small frame on the wall, was a black-and-white photograph of the animal. The twine and hook from which it hung were visible above. At first it didn't register. I glanced at it, then walked away and began buttoning my raincoat against the elements. But something made me turn back to take a second look at the photograph and, sure enough, there was *Killer*, last of the Tasmanian Tigers. I had expected a massively muscled, striped creature with blazing eyes and giant paws. *Killer* was more like a greyhound or a coyote than a tiger. Her fur was short, with patches of mange showing on one flank. Her low-hanging tail, mottled with white, resembled a spindly tree branch. Her foxlike face was looking directly at the camera, her small dark eyes staring up at the lens, her head cocked; it was as if she was pleading for the answer to a question she could not voice. She had no idea that all her kin had vanished. Forever.

The caption under the photograph was hardly legible, and the glue had long ago given out so that the edges were brown and curling back on themselves.

> *Killer, last of the Tasmanian Tigers, photographed at Hobart zoo in 1936, just before her death. Unique to Tasmania, the Tasmanian Tiger once roamed the entire territory. A placid animal trustful of humans, the Tiger was widely hunted for sport, (although its coat was of no commercial value, and its meat had the flavor of dog).*

> *The last five known specimens were captured for exhibition at Crowley's Famous Circus but proved to be a disappointment to*

patrons who expected the fiercer, more romantic beast the name
'Tiger' suggests. Four of the five were put down, and Killer lived
out her last seven years in solitary captivity at Hobart Zoo.

I paused to study the photograph more closely. Something at the back of Killer's cage caught my eye. Propped against the wire mesh was a giant mirror. Perhaps the zookeeper had realized that this was the only place Killer would ever see another of its kind; perhaps, through those seven years, this had helped keep Killer from giving up.

By the time I got back to America, I already knew I had lost Tracy. It was nothing specific, just her voice on the phone the last few times; that and a feeling I carried with me out of the museum in Hobart. She met me at the airport. Her brother was with her. We hugged, but didn't kiss.

When we got to the house, she didn't come in. She said, "You'd best be left alone. You've got a lot of adjusting to do."

I knew she didn't mean jet lag.

I let myself in and ambled from room to room. In the bathroom, on the floor beside the shower door, a towel still lay where I had dropped it six months before as I had raced to make the plane.

The house was no longer a home. It was just me in an empty building.

And I was the sole survivor.

Chapter 30
Stretching Time

O NE YEAR, WHEN NATALIE was nine and Rex was five, I made a giant ruler out of cardboard and pinned it against our kitchen wall.

The kids marked each other's height in pencil in their careful, messy scrawls, concentrating hard. After that, we held measuring days at regular intervals.

Natalie would say, "Rex! Don't. Dad lookit! Rex is standing on tippytoes."

And Rex would say, "No I am not, dad! Nat's a fibber."

Even then, I knew I wanted more than anything to make those years last for longer than they would.

I can remember listening to the two little voices echo around the house and closing my eyes, imagining how empty the world would feel after they had grown up and gone.

Now that they have, it feels exactly like I'd imagined.

PART FIVE

HURDLES AND HOPES

TIME HEALS

Chapter 31

Boundaries

If you touch me there

she said,

I will lash out.

That part of me is private.

Chapter 32

Patience

Your mother says that patience is a virtue

She lies.

It stifles you in sweaty classrooms

the bursting mown-grass breeze of May

beckons through the windows' cracks

with scented fingers stirring folds of flowered fabric

on your flimsy cotton dress,

the one that cost ten dollars from Penny's discount rack

your mother steered you to.

As girl gives way to woman,

the keepers of your world

tie up your wings with ropes

and gag your mouth.

The teachers in your head still tease the pupil,

who has long outgrown their droning yawning mantras;

their fingers hold the rope that hangs

under the recess bell

but never let it ring.

Too much.

Too long.

Too small.

You squeeze between the bars

and soar away

the nagging, pleading voices

fading as you fly.

A raptor, ravenous and resolute

with nothing on your mind

except the urges that you feel.

Chapter 33

Shame

I WAS BORN IN 1954, and raised in postwar London
The women in my life have been champions of the underdog. In many ways, they are my heroes.

My grandmother fought against child labor and the practice of having pregnant women work sixteen hour shifts until they reached full term. She won the fight.

My grandfather died three months after my mother was born, so there were no men in the house as she grew up. In 1943 she was a teenager living in Glasgow, when the Germans blitz-bombed the city. My mother hid under the staircase as the bombs reduced neighboring houses to rubble. In her 60s she volunteered to teach in a school in London's slums, where violence and drugs were the everyday backdrop. One day a girl in the school broke a chair over the principal's head and fractured her skull.

I am at a writers' workshop in Northern California. Six hundred women and three men. It is a three-day class for memoir writers. I had not known that so few men would attend. Elizabeth Gilbert (*Eat Pray Love*) and

Cheryl Strayed (*Wild*) are the moderators, two authors that I revere and whose works hypnotize with their raw power.

It occurs to me that I am one third of one percent of the participants, but I represent forty-nine percent of the US population. I feel embarrassed; an unwanted misfit, and looking around I guess I am one of the oldest people there. I make myself small, hiding, and unwanted.

Over three days, I hear the stories of dozens of lives, told by women from all backgrounds, old and young, voicing tales of womanhood in a hostile world. These are not activists, crusaders, missionaries for a cause. They are, simply, the fifty-one percent who have found a safe place to share their voices and their truths. One by one, encouraged by Gilbert and Strayed, they stand up, nervous and naked, unable, often, to speak without sobbing and shaking. As the stories unfold, I learn of lives stunted by prejudice, silenced by bosses, colleagues, and husbands, and of lives destroyed by assaults, on the body and on the spirit.

Often, we are asked to turn to the person next to us, or behind us, and share our stories for comment and feedback. I am British by birth, and as I turn around to the woman behind me (I will call her 'J' for the purpose of this story). I feel her spirit sink, and (I imagine) recoil. When it is her turn to share her experiences, she says to me:

"Forgive me. When I heard your accent and saw you were an older man, a memory flooded over me. It was a memory I have spent many years trying to shake, but it lurks just beneath the surface, like a tentacle ready to pull me under and drown me." Her face had tightened, and her eyes glowered as she spoke. "I was once an overseas student at Oxford University. I was young and full of hope and excited to be in the country I had always wanted to visit." She paused. One beautiful evening, I went for a walk across the time worn cobblestones, past the fawn-colored stones of the 16th century colleges and chapels. It was early summertime." Her face took on a dreamy, faraway expression. "I remember the swans on the Thames, gliding, white, placid. The scent rising from the sunkissed surface of the cooling water." Her brow relaxed. "The sun was setting as I walked along a small lane that led to a hidden church with a graveyard. Headstones told tales of long-ago lives, many cut short for reasons unknown. I strolled around to the back of the church where the oldest graves were placed, worn and moss covered."

She has taken me with her. I feel a sense of peace and safety, back there in my homeland, familiar still after fifty years. I can picture the church, which was like so many I had been in, attending evensong and being grateful for my faith.

Her expression changes, suddenly. Utterly. "From an entrance at the side of the church, I saw an old man shuffle toward me. I thought he was going to ask me a question or perhaps share a story about the history of the church or the graves. Then something about his walk, the quickening of his pace, made me uncomfortable. He lurched forward and lunged at me. His breath was sour, and his teeth were yellow and rotten. He pushed me over and fell on me. He was heavy and strong. The rest is a blur. When he released me, I ran. I felt ashamed, and that somehow it was my fault. I am still ashamed." She is sobbing now, breathing in, and gasping as she cries.

I don't remember what I said exactly, but I do know that I expressed sorrow. I wanted more than anything to take the trouble from her eyes. I wanted to hunt down the old man and punish him. I remember saying that as a man, I could only try to tell her that there were good men, kind men, men who honor women and who would defend, champion, and support her and all women; men who would lead with honesty, with vulnerability and tenderness.

She asks if we can exchange addresses, which we did.

During a break, I use the men's bathroom, which is empty. When I come out, I hear a commotion in the hallway and see a long line of women waiting to get into the women's bathroom. I suggest to the women at the back of the line that they might like to use the men's bathroom and that I will stand at the entrance for them to ensure that no man would go in. I absolutely do not want any credit for this. It just maked logical sense. The women move down the corridor to the men's bathroom and use it in turn. I stand with my back to the entrance to make sure that my two fellow men will know to use the men's bathroom across the courtyard in the dining room. I know they will understand. At some point a maintenance engineer for the conference center heads for the front of the line to the men's bathroom and asks the woman first in line to step aside as it is the men's and tells her she should go to the women's bathroom. I ask him politely to consider using the bathroom across the courtyard, as the women's' bathroom is too full to accommodate all the attendees. He argues with me to the point where it becomes unpleasant, but eventually he gives up and stomps away.

At the end of the three days, Cheryl and Elizabeth encourage individuals to step up to the microphone and ask questions, or simply say something that is important to them.

One-by-one women come forward and, mostly, summarize the important experiences that they would include in their memoirs if they found the time (or the courage) to write them. Time after time I hear about the real lives of actual women. Some of the voices are sad, some frightening, some angry, and some hopeful.

Toward the end of the question-and-answer session, I decide there is something I simply have to say. When my turn comes, I address the room, and particularly Elizabeth Gilbert and Cheryl Strayed. "I am a man." Laughter ripples through the audience. "I am honored and humbled, truly, to hear your stories and to be entrusted with glimpses into the private lives of so many women. I am in awe of your intelligence, vulnerability, eloquence, and sincerity. My overwhelming feeling is that I'm ashamed of being a man." The room grows silent. "I am not perfect, but I do hope that I have lived a decent and respectful life in my relationships with women. However, I also recognize that many of us men and many of our predecessors have contributed greatly to the sadness, and in many cases to the horrors, encountered by so many women. The only thing that I can say is that good men do exist, and so very many of us are ashamed and angry. On behalf of men, I apologize for what so many of us have put you through."

I return to my seat. I am embarrassed. I feel like they will think I am looking for credit, to show myself as better than other men. It is the opposite, but that is how I feel. I reflect and tell myself that I have at least spoken my mind. What follows truly humbles me. At first, some faint applause begins but then rises until the entire room is clapping. I feel unworthy and embarrassed. Cheryl Strayed presses one hand against her heart, and waits for the applause to fade, and then addresses me directly.

"I am so very saddened to know that you are ashamed to be a man." Her voice quavers and she has tears in her eyes. I want you to know that you are not alone; so many men share the admiration and respect you have for us women. You need to know also that for men it is not all roses either. You would never be comfortable saying this, so I will do so for you: In a family unit, when a woman says, 'You know what? I'd like to stop working and pursue my passion for writing, sailing, taking courses in painting, cooking, mountaineering, exploring my spirituality', (fill in the blank) it is typically perfectly acceptable, and the man is left being the sole contributor to the family's financial wellbeing. On the other hand, typically, if a man says the same thing to his working spouse the acceptance is often grudging at best and, at worst, non-existent."

The next thing that happens is that one of the two other men in the room takes the microphone.

"You have just expressed what I was thinking. I applaud you for the admiration you have for women and the anger you have for how many of our fellow men have behaved."

When the session is over and we all file out of the auditorium, several women come up to me and thank me for being an ally, and for speaking up. I drive home that evening, feeling a combination of sadness and warmth of spirit.

A few weeks later, an envelope arrives in the mail. I do not recognize the handwriting on the address. Inside there is a note (I still have it). There is no phone number. It reads:

> *Alan, I have to tell you that you restored a part of me that I thought I had lost forever. Your words and your spirit and your understanding–I will cherish these and hold them close in moments of doubt and fear. Thank you.*
>
> *J*

Chapter 34

Borrowing Youth

I T WAS THIRTY YEARS since I had borrowed anything without permission, but the red Schwinn bicycle was just sitting there, and no one was around. I would have it back before they knew it was gone. Swinging my leg over the saddle, I pushed hard against the sidewalk with one foot and was away.

It was a 1964 short frame Schwinn Stingray, low to the ground so you could drag your knee on the pavement when you cornered. Chrome fenders, 2-speed gear hub, sprung forks. The Stingray was built a full five years before the movie *Easy Rider* was released, but it was a motorless version of the famous *chopper* that the hippie Peter Fonda rode.

I straddled the long, ribbed, *banana* seat cushion and leant back against the trademark high loop strut. I put my hands on the red rubber grips with their long tassels, one either side of the two-foot-high *ape-hanger* handlebars. As a kid, the bars had been so high that I could only reach them once I was in the saddle. Now I had to hunch over to grip them, and the seat was too low to allow my legs to straighten.

It didn't matter. I forgot for a moment that there were no brake levers on the handlebars and then remembered that the pedals were the brakes; you just had to apply reverse pressure on them and the bike would slow down–or more typically, skid to a halt.

The acacia-scented wind in my face and the spring sun glinting off the chrome horn on the handlebars. It was a time before girls, cigarettes, and money; a time of bubble gum and Spiderman comics and hiding them from mom. These were the days of turning corners on unfamiliar streets just to see what was around them.

The wide whitewall tires hummed on the sidewalk, and for a moment I really was ten again.

Chapter 35

Fireflies in the Dark

Electing the Dictator

The election's over and the tyrant won.

The alarm still echoes, bouncing off the walls

that separate the people in our land.

Through countless bedroom windows

moonlight's fingers stroke the faces

of exhaustion and defiance.

We dreamers wonder if our dreams were nightmares

and yawn and leave our bedrooms to find out.

One by one we dreamers step outside.

Under our feet, the losing voting ballots rustle

like yellowed leaves in the November wind.

From trains and cars, five million people pour

onto the streets beside us as we walk.

From South and East and North

and from the middle of the land they love.

From left and right and center

And nobody is wrong.

They join dawn's chorus in the streets outside,

just murmured voices, faint at first,

then, slowly, as they join,

the sound turns into singing.

All we are saying is give peace a chance.

A juggernaut of girls and boys and men and women run,

a flaming torch in every outstretched hand

and line the roads and marvel at our future

as we gather speed towards the coming day.

At last, up front, a raised hand signals.

One hundred Million fireflies stop and gather.

Our sweat sends steam into the winter chill.

Dawn holds its breath.

We runners squint into the early light

and crowd onto a massive stage.

Our multicolored faces offer simple kindness.

The torches flicker

and we hold each other's hands.

Chapter 36

Fragile

Tread away from the edge;

it matters

if we fall.

Lovers' hearts and rainbows' curves

and children's hopeful souls,

the wing of a moth and the nose of a fawn

and the light of the sun in its westerly bath.

Cradle your arms, cradle your arms,

shelter your cubs in the eye of the storm;

it matters if they perish.

The clearest sky we ever knew,

and the perfectly formed spider's web in the dew,

the skin of a peach and the full field of wheat

and the kiss in the dark after ages apart.

Don't crush it or fold it or lose it or scold it,

don't leave it outside in the snow;

it's only a shadow, a glimpse, and a wish.

A seed with a choice of soil.

About the Author

Alan Collenette is a San Francisco Bay Area author and a Scottish expatriate. His short stories, poetry, essays and articles have appeared in *Bust Out, San Francisco Business Times, The Registry* and in *Writers Digest* where he received Honorable Mentions in the 71st Annual Competition in the Genre Short Story and Literary Short Story categories and was named Award Winner in the *Pacific Sun Writers Competition.*

Love Brain & Other Minefields features a mix of award-winning poetry and short stories where women are revered, and love is both a sanctuary and a minefield for unsuspecting men. Loss lingers like an echo and musings drift between harsh reality and absurdity. Alan Collenette weaves moments of sharp insight and lyrical grace into every page.

Coming in 2027

Immortal – The Two Lives of John Paul Jones

Alan Collenette's next book is a historical novel based on the life of John Paul Jones, the legendary Scotsman who founded the US Navy. The following is an excerpt from the book.

EXCERPT

Immortal – The Two Lives of John Paul Jones

It is Indian summer in the north of England. A full moon has ushered in a warm, windless night, and the North Sea stretches out in front of the awestruck audience on the clifftops. For these onlookers, it is as though they are witnessing a tragedy of ancient design: a valiant underdog locked in mortal struggle with a monstrous adversary. Now, as the final act unfolds, the crowd is hushed, transfixed by the spectacle of a hero's last agony. The American ship is ablaze. Little more than a funeral pyre adrift on the sea, the remains of her torn canvas are being devoured by flames, one of her three masts has been demolished, and cannon fire has torn a huge gash in her side. She is sinking.

Captain John Paul Jones is standing on the quarterdeck of his doomed ship, his face black with soot and his white jacket spattered with blood and tar. He estimates it will be less than an hour before she goes down. The aging merchant ship - hastily converted for war - has been no match for the British frigate, fast, purpose-built, and with cannon power vastly superior to his own. His surgeon's grim report nags at his conscience; more than a hundred and fifty men are either dead or mortally wounded. A gruesome mixture of seawater, severed limbs, and bilge water swirls around his ankles. The First Officer is standing beside him, and has to shout to make himself heard above the roar of cannon fire and the howls of dying men, "Captain Jones, Sir, our fate is decided. I request permission to yield." Jones looks at him, as if considering the question. He does not reply.

The suggestion lingers in the smoke-laden air. A few moments pass, and the officer asks again, "Sir, may I have your permission to strike our colors?" - Lowering the flag would signify surrender.

A familiar calm settles over him. Surrender has not even entered Jones's mind. Time pauses, as if death itself is granting him one last opportunity to survey the scene. He thinks of the lives lost over his thirty-three years; ten-year-old cabin boys, thousands of miles from home; countless sailors, and the families who will never see them again. How will history judge him, if it remembers him at all? There is so much left undone. He turns toward the officer, puts one arm on each of his shoulders and glares into his face. "No, sir, I will do no such thing. Return to your post."

As the officer turns to leave, Jones seizes his elbow, spinning him back around. Their faces nearly touch, Jones's hat knocking the officer's to the blood-soaked deck. Amidst the cacophony of cannon fire and musket shot, Jones's voice is low but unwavering. "If you so much as breathe that suggestion to a single man, you will not live to see our victory."

***

To learn more visit www.alancollenette.com

Follow on Facebook at www.facebook.com/alancollenette

Publishing Credits

THESE STORIES AND POEMS by Alan Collenette have previously appeared elsewhere:

- *Mister Speedy* originally published in the print edition of *Bust Out*, Vol. 2 No. 5, Winter Issue (ISSN 1084-9084)

- *Ingling* originally published in the print edition of *Bust Out*, Vol. 4 No. 10, Spring Issue (ISSN 1084-9084)

- *Paradise Motors* originally published in the print edition of *Bust Out*, Vol. 3 No. 6, Summer Issue (ISSN 1084-9084)

- *Bottom Land* originally published in the print edition of *Bust Out* Vol. 1 No. 3, Spring Issue (ISSN 1084-9084)

- *Scent* originally published in the print edition of *Writers Digest* and received Honorable Mentions in the 71st Annual Competition in the Genre Short Story

- *The Lucky Tie* originally in the print edition of the *San Francisco*

Business Times (October, 2001 – Tribute to 911)

- *Something Lost* published in the print edition of *Writers Digest* and received Honorable Mention in the 71st Annual Competition in the Mainstream / Literary Short Story Category

- *Her Spare Hand* named Award Winner with monetary compensation in the *Pacific Sun Writers Competition*

- *Gray* originally published in the print edition of *Bust Out*, Vol. 1 No 2. Fall Issue (ISSN 1084-9084)

- *Angelface* originally published in the print edition of *Bust Out*, Vol. 2 No 4. Summer/Fall Issue (ISSN 1084-9084)